Dragon Blood 5: Mage

Dragon Blood 5
Mage

Avril Sabine

Cracked Acorn Productions
Australia

Dragon Blood 5: Mage

Published by

Cracked Acorn Productions

PO Box 1365

Gympie, Queensland 4570

Australia

978-1-925131-31-4 (Kindle)

978-1-925617-66-5 (EPUB)

978-1-925131-42-0 (Print)

Genre: Young Adult Urban Fantasy

Just like the others, it's for you three again.

Amber wants to take back control of her life. She's fed up with assassins, death threats, unrealistic expectations, nightmares and secrets. The secrets most of all. Especially Ronan's secrets and in particular his secret that she knows will scare the hell out of her and will probably never let her have another moment of peace. Maybe some secrets shouldn't be told.

*

This story was written by an Australian author using Australian spelling.

Name Pronunciation

Like many names there is more than one way to pronounce the following ones. These are the pronunciations used in this series.

Names:

Alsandair (ahl–san–dare)

Anrai (arn–ree)

Bredon (bread–en)

Chait (single syllable, rhymes with hate)

Daray (dah–ray)

Doneele (donny–lee)

Emlyn (em–lin)

Gair (rhymes with hair)

Gethin (geh-thin)

Isleen (ish-lean)

Kiani (key-ah-knee)

Laren (lah-rin)

Maira (may-rah)

Orin (oh-rin)

Paili (pah-lee)

Queran (qwhere-rin)

Rhobert (row-bert)

Rian (ree-in)

Ronan (row-nen)

Tahmid (tar-mid)

Turi (two-ree)

Other pronunciations:

Erilan (era-len)

Feralenzi (fair-a-len-zee)

Pliethin (plea-thin)

Temolae (tem-oh-lay)

Chapter One

Amber wrapped the tiny unicorn statue in tissue paper, smiling at the little girl who bounced on the spot, her hands clasped tightly together. She looked over towards the young boy who was looking between a statue of a dragon and one of a knight.

"Can't I get both, Mum?"

The woman shook her head. "No. If you can't make up your mind in the next ten seconds you're going to miss out."

"But they're friends. How can I take one home without the other?" the boy asked.

His mother grinned. "Nice try. Now pick one. You're running out of time."

Amber was tempted to tell him that dragons and knights weren't friends. All they wanted to do was kill each other. Instead, she kept her smile in place and took the dragon statue the boy handed her, wrapping it in tissue paper before ringing up the purchases.

When the family left the shop, she sighed, her smile fading. It was probably the worst job she could've taken, but there hadn't been many choices and out of all the ones she'd applied for it had been the only one that had accepted her. If it hadn't been for all the dragon statues constantly reminding her of how much she missed Kade, working in the gift shop would have been a breeze.

Amber spun at a sound behind her. When she saw it was her boss, Monica, coming out of the staff area, she was relieved she'd finally learned not to raise her hands to attack. She smiled slightly and started to turn back to the front of the shop.

"Amber, do you have anything planned for late this afternoon?"

She shook her head. "No. Why?"

"A shipment I was expecting to arrive before five won't be here until nearly six. If it was any other day it wouldn't matter, but it's my niece's tenth birthday and I can't be late to her party. She might forgive me, but my daughter never would. That pair are inseparable."

Amber shrugged. "I guess so." Once her and Crystal had been inseparable. Now she couldn't even bring herself to ring Crystal. There were so many things they couldn't talk about.

"Are you certain? It won't be difficult. All you'll need to do is sign for the shipment and show them where to put the boxes in the storage area. We can unpack them tomorrow."

Six would be fine. It was still bright enough for her to walk home at that hour. And it wasn't like she had anything else planned for her night. Once Friday night would have meant doing something. Not anymore. "It's not a problem." The overtime would be good. She hated having to use the money Rian had put into a bank account for her. It felt like cheating.

Monica grinned. "There's no one you have to check with? A boyfriend maybe?"

She managed to keep her expression neutral. When would she stop feeling this wrenching pain every time she thought of him? It had been nine weeks and five days. Surely it shouldn't be so bad by now. At least she'd stopped counting the amount of hours. "I'll send my housemates a text to let them know I'll be late." Elliot wouldn't care, but Cooper would panic if she didn't turn up on time.

The shop door opened and three girls walked in, talking and laughing. Monica nodded towards them.

"I'll take care of this lot while you send that text. And thanks. I don't know how I'd manage without you."

Amber watched Monica weave her way through the display shelves, cheerfully greeting the girls. Escaping to the staff room, she dropped onto a chair at the small round table in the cramped kitchenette, taking her phone from her pocket. She stared at the blank screen, tempted to ring Kade, or even Crystal. But she couldn't. Not without becoming the killer Ronan had been trying to force her to become. Before she gave in, she quickly sent both Elliot and Cooper a message telling them she had to work late. Only Cooper replied.

Do you want me to pick you up?

She sighed heavily, wondering when he'd stop mothering her. *No.* She'd have plenty of time to get home before it was dark. Three quarters of an hour. And she would have been home long before dark, but the delivery was even later than expected. It wasn't until seven that she was locking up the shop and striding towards home, wondering if she should call Cooper and tell him to come and pick her up.

Turning down a side street, she decided it wasn't that far. Ten minutes walk. What could happen in ten minutes on quiet backstreets? Nothing. There was no one around. She resisted the urge to mentally search the area. That wasn't her. This was her new life. How could she expect to make a go of her new life if she automatically kept trying to use the skills of her old one?

She ignored the hollow feeling and the little voice that told her it wasn't much of a life. So she was still sorting it out. Her job was okay. The house she shared with Elliot and Cooper wasn't bad, only a short walk to the beach, and who could complain about living on the Sunshine Coast? Probably her grandmother, but she wasn't going to think about her.

Thoughts of Kade crept in. Or think about him either. They were all part of her old life. The one that wasn't hers. She turned into yet another street, freezing when she heard a woman scream. Halfway down the street she saw two men, a woman almost hidden by their figures. Adrenaline and instinct kicked in and she raced forward, the men spinning to face her.

A gun was aimed directly at her and she saw the woman backing away. "Run!" Before the man with the gun could turn and stop the woman, Amber covered the last of the distance between them, her fist connecting with his jaw, the gun going off. She twisted to the side, the bullet flying past her.

The other man attacked and she blocked, spinning around behind him, punching him low in the back, remembering how once there would have been a dagger in her hand by now. For a moment she thought she caught the scent of a dragon, then it was gone. She mentally searched the area. The woman was nearly at the end of the street. A few of the houses nearby had people and she hoped none of them called the police.

Her fists flew as she dodged, spun and resisted the urge to change her form. The last thing she needed was to be standing naked in the street when she became human again. Her heart raced, her senses were all alert and neither of the men could touch her. They weren't fast enough. Then it was only one of them. And shortly he was lying on the bitumen, not far from his companion who was sprawled half on the grassed footpath and half in the gutter.

Amber stared at the two men. "What the hell was I thinking?" She'd left Kade to escape this. It was all around her. All she'd done was stop fighting for the weak. Stopped looking out for those she loved. This was the first time she'd felt alive in nine weeks and five days. The first moment in all that time when she'd felt like herself.

In the distance she heard sirens. How on earth was

she going to explain this? She pulled out her phone and dialled Ronan's number. Her call was sent, mid ring, to his message bank. Was that it? Had she left it too long to ring him? Relief rushed through her when he stepped out of the Void in front of her.

"Nice work." He nodded towards the men lying at her feet.

"What am I going to tell the cops?"

"Nothing." He grinned. "You won't be here to tell them anything." He raised his voice. "Chait. Daray. Get out here."

The two Golds stepped out of the Void, both nodding towards Amber in greeting before they turned their attention on Ronan.

"Dump these men somewhere else and see that the area is cleaned up." Ronan held out his hand to Amber when the two Golds disappeared with the men.

"Daray came out of the Void when I was fighting." She took his hand, letting him take her through the Void and to his rooftop water garden. It almost felt like coming home. How crazy was that?

"I dragged him back into the Void. He's yours by the way. Your second warrior. He's useless to me. No matter what task I sent him on he always had to check that you were okay. It was easier just to set him to watching over you rather than wasting the time of the other Gold I had watching you from the Void."

"I don't need a second warrior." The protest was automatic.

Ronan laughed. "Still playing games, kitten?"

She stared at him, meeting his gold eyes. Everything else about him looked the same. His hair was darker than the white blond she knew it to be, he was taller than his real height which was only a little above her own height and he looked to be in his thirties rather than barely twenty. "Looks like I'm not the only one playing games. Only your eyes show what you truly look like."

Ronan's predatory smile formed. "They know what I look like. They've seen my true colours."

"Really? Your true colours? Which true colours? The ones that somehow you're Gold or the ones that you're a bastard who's only out for himself?"

Again Ronan laughed. "I've missed you, kitten." He held up his hand, palm out to the side of him and Anrai stepped out of the Void, giving Ronan a small bundle of dragon-leather before he disappeared.

Amber's eyes narrowed as she realised it was her daggers and their sheaths that she'd shoved in the back of her wardrobe. "I hope Anrai didn't upset Cooper by turning up like that."

"Cooper wouldn't have known he was there." Ronan held out the daggers. "Are you going to take them?"

She continued to meet his gaze. "I'm not yours to order around."

"But are you mine?"

She hesitated. She checked the link she'd created to make sure she'd always be able to find him. It was as strong as ever. Her automatic response was no, but instinct overrode that and prevented what she guessed would have been the worst mistake she could have made. "A better question to ask is, are you mine?" She had to be smarter this time. It was going to be on her terms. No one else's.

"It's certainly an interesting question. Probably has the same answer as the question I asked you."

She racked her brain for an answer. Not once in the past nine weeks and five days had she been forced to think this carefully about a decision. She grinned, surprised at how much she'd missed it. "I must be crazy."

"That's never been in doubt, kitten. What is in doubt is if you're mine."

"It's such an awful term in my world. And we currently are in my world. It speaks of ownership and slavery."

"Should I take you to my world and ask you again? In my world it speaks of who you'll protect, who you'll stand by. Who you won't go against. More than an ally. More than family and more than a lover. Last time, Amber. Are you mine?"

She'd never seen him so serious. Not even those times when he was close to death. She took the daggers he still held. "I am as much yours as you are mine. I won't go against you, Ronan. Not because we're allies, not because we're something that is neither friends or enemies and not because you're the oldest dragon in existence and could probably teach me everything I need to know about surviving." Still holding his gaze, she slid her hands into the dagger sheaths and tightened them around her wrists.

"Then why?"

"Because I'm human and we tend to have these irrational emotions that make no sense. And I trust you with me. No one else, just me. I trust that for some reason, which would probably make no sense to me at all, that you will protect me, that you will stand by me and you won't go against me. And not just because you gave me your word."

"You're right, you wouldn't understand why."

"Are you going to tell me?"

He stared at her for a minute. *"I had begun to think*

I would outlive everyone." He held out his hand. "Time to go."

Amber took his hand, knowing better than to ask him exactly what he meant. He had obviously told her as much as he was going to. And far more than she'd expected. "Where are we going?" They came out of the Void into a modern bedroom and after a quick mental search, she realised they were still in Ronan's house. "I want to see Kade."

"Eventually." Ronan gestured towards the dragon-leather clothes on the bed. "Get dressed. I'll be back in ten minutes." He vanished.

A search showed he'd returned to his rooftop garden. Amber sighed. This wasn't exactly taking control of her life. *"Don't think you can always tell me what to do."*

"You're wasting time."

Muttering under her breath about dragons, she changed into the black dragon-leather trousers and vest. The clothes felt so familiar and as comfortable as her own skin. She closed her eyes, her hand going to where a sword should hang. Breathing in she smiled slightly at the familiar scent of dragon-leather.

She'd needed the time away. Needed to get some perspective after all that had happened. There was a lot she hated, so much she never wanted to relive, but so much more that she loved. Things that made her feel alive, that made her blood sing in her veins. She lifted her hand, opening her eyes to watch a fireball form in her palm. Her smile widened as she closed her hand, extinguishing the flames. This time was going to be different. She could handle it. The alternative wasn't acceptable. The pain she normally felt when she thought of Kade was pushed away by anticipation.

"I'm ready. I want to see Kade now."

Instead of answering, Ronan appeared in front of her, grabbing her hand and taking her through the Void.

Chapter Two

When Ronan let go of her hand, Amber looked around, surprised by their surroundings. "Your family crypt? Why've you brought me here?" She watched as he removed one of the stones from the wall, the scent of the long dead filling the area.

He held out a journal. The dark brown, leather cover looked new. "Read this."

"Now?" She eyed the journal. From the loose pages that she could see at regular intervals, it looked like most of the pages were filled. "I'm not that fast a reader."

"Just take the damn book."

She reluctantly took it, holding it against her chest.

"You're wearing through my patience. Open it up, Amber."

Hearing him speak her name made her want to look inside even less. "You only told me I had to take it for now." It must be pretty important if this was the first thing he wanted her to see when she returned. And she had a really bad feeling about it. Worse than any of the other bad feelings she'd ever had.

Ronan stared at her a moment before his predatory smile formed. "I had no idea you wanted to spend the night in my family crypt with me. Why don't I go and get a couple of chairs for us to sit on? I won't be too long."

Still holding the journal against her chest, she reached out with her other hand to capture his arm. "Don't you dare leave me in here. And don't threaten me. I want to see Kade before I do anything else."

"One page. Look at the first page and afterwards, I'll take you to Kade."

She held his gaze a moment longer before she let go of his arm. Opening the journal to the first page she stared at it, the word 'no' ringing in her mind. Closing her eyes, she slammed the book shut. The image reminded her of the wooden bench in Ronan's foyer. She remembered the first time she'd seen it. The day they'd captured his castle. It was made from a dark timber, the legs carved in the shape of nightmare-like creatures, their prey dead at their feet. Their human prey. And she'd asked him whose it was only to learn it was as old as his castle.

"Kitten?"

She shook her head, her eyes still closed, the journal pressed against her chest, one hand raised to stop his words. Did she really want to know what it was all about? Did she really… she stopped mid thought and her eyes flew open, her mouth gaping as she recalled Vikki's last moments. "The hounds are coming."

Ronan nodded.

"I thought she was talking about your son. Why would you name your son after these?"

"A Hound to catch a hound."

"What are they?"

"When humans first saw them, they called them demons, evil spirits, but the name that stuck was Hell Hounds."

"The hounds are coming." She spoke the words softly. "Why now? Why are they coming now? What has changed?"

"Nothing has changed. They've always been coming. What the Knights did to keep them out of this world could never last. But they didn't want to believe that."

"What did they do?"

"They bound our worlds together. Ours, the Pliethins' and yours. It kept the Hell Hounds from coming through the Void. When they first bound our worlds, it lasted a century, but now each binding is lucky to last a decade."

"What has this got to do with us?"

"Look at that picture again, kitten." When she continued to leave the book closed, Ronan gestured towards it. "Go on, open it up."

She reluctantly opened the book and stared at the picture. It was a photocopy of a hand drawing. The markings faded and smudged in places. "Who drew this?"

"My grandfather. He was the first one to tell them that their plan wouldn't work. And when I saw everything he'd learned, and read some of the information he'd written down, I knew he was right. But they wouldn't listen to me either. I was only a child."

She could easily imagine how that would have annoyed him. "But surely someone else must have realised?"

"If they did, they didn't want to know about it or do anything about it. The binding is what caused the fall out between the Knights, mages and dragons. They didn't have to sacrifice anyone. Only the dragons did. And at first the Dragon Mages were sacrificed too, but they eventually learned how to use Pliethins instead."

"They?"

"The Knights."

"My grandparents know about this?"

Ronan shook his head. "Most people don't know about this. At least not all of it. I'm the only one left alive who knows the full story."

"But all this was ages ago. Maybe it's different now."

"Have you listened to anything I've said? When they first sealed our Voids together it lasted a hundred years. Now, it barely lasts ten years. Eventually it won't hold at all. Look at that picture." He jabbed a finger towards it. "Do you really want something like that coming after your mother?"

She slammed the book shut. There was no way she was about to let anything come after her mother. No dragon, no Knight and certainly not the large fanged creature that looked like an upright, rabid dog. "So all this is because you want to save the world?"

Ronan threw back his head and laughed. "Don't go making a hero out of me, kitten. I'm not hero material. Like I've told you before. This is all about survival. When the binding shatters, if we're not prepared, those hounds will destroy our worlds and everyone in them."

She remembered him telling her, months ago, that

he'd leave his journals to her if he died. "Is all this in your journals?"

Ronan nodded. "Yes."

"Where are they? Your journals. You told me the journals were mine if you died. So where have you hidden them?"

He held her gaze a moment longer before nodding to the place in the wall where he'd replaced the stone. "In there." His expression hardened. "If you read them before I die you are asking me to kill you. Understand?"

She nodded, knowing it was a promise he'd keep. "So you wanted to make sure someone would deal with this even if you couldn't. I thought you said you were no hero."

Ronan laughed again. "No. It wasn't about dealing with it. I wanted to make sure they didn't win even if I'd died. None of them listened to me. Or my grandfather. We weren't Gold so we didn't matter."

"Is that why you wanted a Council seat? So they'd listen to you?"

"No. I wanted a Council seat so I could steal back my grandfather's notes that they'd taken. I wanted to translate them so I could find out where the binding was done. We have to destroy it."

Amber took an involuntary step away from him. "You want to let them in?"

"I want to end this farce so we can get on with doing what should have been done in the first place."

"And what's that?"

"We should have been hunting them down and destroying them instead of letting them breed and grow in strength." He pointed a finger at her. "That's what Dragon Mages were made for. No matter what skin a Hell Hound wears, you can see through it."

"Skin?"

"They can take on the appearance of anyone they have killed and eaten. It's how they gain their strength. And the parents take some of their kills back to their offspring. It's the only way they can grow and strengthen. From the living flesh of other intelligent creatures."

This wasn't what she'd expected to hear when she'd phoned Ronan. Oh, she'd known he was keeping some secret she wasn't going to like, but this, this was so far beyond the realms of normal she didn't know what to think. "Do we have to stay in here?" She was getting sick of being surrounded by death.

"No one will disturb us here and no one can stay in the Void in this crypt." Ronan's predatory smile formed. "It's not the dead you should be worried about."

Amber's arms tightened around the book she clutched to her chest. "Couldn't you at least have given me one day back before you dumped all of this on me?"

"No."

"Why not?"

"Because it's time for you to do your part. I have an army of Golds loyal to me. I need you to make us an army of mages that's loyal to us."

"I thought you didn't want Dragon Mages."

"It wasn't time. Now it is. And I never had an issue with making Dragon Mages. Only making ones that aren't loyal to us."

"I need to think about this."

Ronan gestured towards the book she continued to hug. "Do you want creatures like that loose in your world? Humans are their preferred meal. Most of you are too weak to put up much of a fight. Even against the weakest Hell Hound."

"You can't expect to dump all of this on me and expect me to be ready to go. I need time."

"How much time?"

Amber shrugged. "I don't know. I have to give my boss notice. And give her time to replace me."

"Tell her you quit and you won't be back Monday."

"I can't quit my job like that."

"Tell your boss your mum is suffering a breakdown." Ronan grinned. "I'm sure she'll understand."

Amber's eyes narrowed as she recalled her boss talking about the time she'd had to help a friend through a breakdown. "How often were you watching me?"

"Not often. You were far too boring with your frequent sighs and your disinterest in doing anything even remotely interesting."

"I hope you don't expect me to apologise."

Ronan chuckled, gesturing towards her. "This is the person who has been missing for the last couple of months. Try and tell me this isn't you."

She held his gaze a moment longer, the continual gold colour in his eyes unfamiliar. "Why did you think I'd return?"

"Because I know you. As much as you tried to deny it, you are a warrior." When she started to speak he interrupted. "Not a killer, or an assassin, or any other term you might come up with that has a negative meaning in your mind. Everything you've done told me it'd be impossible for you not to want to come back and protect your people. You just had to figure it out for yourself."

She continued to stare at him until she finally nodded. "Will you take me to see Kade now?"

"How much time do you need?"

"To visit him?"

"No, to think about the hounds."

She shrugged. "I don't know. A couple of days, I guess."

He reached for her, taking her through the Void and arriving in the courtyard of Temolae Keep. "Where is he?"

Amber mentally searched for him. "In our room."

Ronan again took her through the Void, but this time when they came out, two unknown Golds stepped out of the Void just after them, swords drawn.

Kade, who'd been asleep in his bed, became human again, rolling out of bed, reaching for a sword leaning against the chest of drawers at the side of the bed. "Amber?"

She took a step away from Ronan, keeping a wary eye on the Golds.

Kade glanced towards the two warriors. "Put your weapons away, light some lamps and get out of here." He leaned the sword against the chest of drawers.

Emotion overwhelmed her and she wanted to fling herself at him and beg him never to let her go again, but she was conscious of Ronan watching them. "We didn't go to schoolies. You owe me a date."

With a laugh Kade strode towards her, taking the book from her arms and tossing it onto the bed. "That wasn't my choice." He wrapped his arms around her, pulling her close. *"I missed you. Ronan and Crystal kept telling me to let you be. That you'd come back. I was beginning to think they were wrong."*

"I'm sorry." She didn't want to let him go. Behind her she felt Ronan disappear into the Void.

"Are you staying?"

"Yes."

"For good?"

"Yeah. I had to figure some things out." Her lips met his and she clung to him until her phone rang. She was tempted to ignore it, but no one called her this late at night. Not unless there was a problem. With one arm still tightly around Kade's waist, she checked her phone, swearing when she saw it was Cooper. "Yeah?"

"Are you okay? I know you said you'd be late, but..." his voice trailed off.

She'd forgotten about him. She should have rung

earlier and let him know what was going on. "I'm with Kade."

"You're going back? You said you were finished with being a mage."

"Well obviously I haven't."

"Does this mean we have to go back to being mages too?"

"No. Look, can we talk about this tomorrow?"

"Is it safe to stay here?"

"Yeah."

"You promise?"

"Look, it's safe, okay?" She'd make sure of it by asking Rian to organise a Gold to keep an eye on Elliot and Cooper.

"Okay. I'll talk to you tomorrow."

She was tempted to turn off her phone before she returned it to her pocket, but that should be the last call for the night. Smiling, she met Kade's gaze. "So where were we?"

"You were about to beg me to forgive you for taking off like that."

Amber laughed, sliding her other arm around his waist. "Really?" Her lips were a breath away from his. "I'm not quite sure how this begging thing works, so you let me know if I'm getting close." She lightly touched her lips to his.

"I reckon this might be fairly close."

She didn't care if it was or not. She wasn't about to let him go for ages.

Chapter Three

The bedroom door being flung open, woke Amber the next morning. She grinned when she saw Crystal in the doorway. Beside her Kade, who'd just turned human, groaned.

With a squeal, Crystal launched herself across the room, throwing herself at Amber. "I thought he was joking when he told me. But Rian never jokes. I can't believe you're here. You're staying now? Oh, I've missed you so much. Well? Are you going to say anything or just grin?"

Amber laughed. "I was waiting for you to take a breath. I forgot for a moment that words are like oxygen for you."

Crystal poked her tongue out before she grabbed Amber's hands. "What are we going to do today? There's so much we need to catch up on."

"Does that mean you're not about to let me get back to sleep?" Kade asked.

"There's no time for sleeping," Crystal said.

Grumbling, Kade staggered out of bed.

Amber drew one of her hands from Crystal, reaching out to Kade. *"We won't be long."*

He took her hand. *"Yeah, right."*

"I'm hungry. I missed dinner last night."

"Then I'll see you shortly for breakfast." He let go of her hand.

Amber nodded, watching him leave the room.

Crystal bounced lightly on the bed to catch Amber's attention. "So what have you been doing? Rian kept telling us you were okay. He said your second warrior was keeping an eye on you."

Second warrior? She was going to have to talk to Rian later. Did he know about Daray? And who'd made that decision? She smiled when Crystal bounced on the bed again when she didn't answer her immediately. "Thinking. I had a lot of thinking to do." Not that she'd done much of it until the last minute.

"You were a bit slow at it. I thought you'd have figured it all out a couple of weeks ago."

Amber laughed. "I missed you. I missed everyone."

"Yeah, well that was your own fault. I can't believe you don't have anything interesting to tell me."

She shrugged. "I didn't do much." Except mope around and miss everyone.

"Well now that you're back, I need you to do something for me."

"What?"

"I want you to talk to Rian."

"What about?"

Crystal glanced around the room before she spoke. "I need you to tell Rian that if I want to hook up with him and he likes me, then there's no problem."

Amber stared at Crystal for a moment. "You like Rian?"

"Yep." Crystal grinned. "Very, very much."

"What about Flinn?"

"I've never liked him that way."

Amber shook her head. "No, I mean about being his mage."

"Oh, I'll continue being his mage. But just because I'm his mage doesn't mean I have to be his girlfriend."

"I didn't expect you to be. Actually, I'm glad you're not. And I'd be even happier if you weren't his mage." She paused. "This won't end well."

"Does that mean you won't tell Rian that there's no problem?"

Amber laughed. "There is a problem. It's called possessive dragons, but I will tell him that the decision is up to the pair of you."

Crystal threw her arms around Amber. "Thank you, thank you, thank you."

Amber tightened her arms around her friend. "I really missed you."

"You were the idiot who took off."

"Yeah, I know." There'd been too much going on. She'd needed time to process it.

Crystal drew away. "So when are you going to talk to Rian?"

"I'm guessing the only answer you'll accept is now."

Crystal nodded emphatically.

"Can't I at least have breakfast first?"

"I suppose so. But you will talk to him straight after that, won't you?"

Nodding, Amber hopped off the bed, grabbed her phone and headed for the door. She'd just about reached it when she decided to turn back and collect the book Ronan had given her. It was lying on the floor half under the bed.

"What's that?" Crystal asked.

"Homework."

"You're studying?"

Amber laughed, shaking her head. "Ronan gave it to me to read."

"But you only got back last night."

"Tell me about it," Amber muttered as they headed out the door.

"What's it about?"

Amber hesitated. Ronan hadn't said she couldn't tell anyone, but he had taken her to his family crypt when he'd told her. "I haven't read it yet. But I'm pretty sure it's probably going to be one of those nightmare inducing type of books."

"It comes from Ronan, that's almost a given, isn't it?"

When they reached the dining room Amber sat beside Kade, leaving the book on her lap as she helped herself to the food in front of her. She sent Ronan a text asking him if she could share the book with her people. He replied almost instantly. *Have you read it?*

Give me a break.

I thought I already had. How long were you gone?

Amber glared at her phone. *I'll read it today. Happy?*

Not even close.

Can they read it after I've read it?

Talk to me first.

She growled, "Bloody dragons."

Kade chuckled, reaching for her hand. "Have you got any plans for the day?"

"Apparently."

"What?"

"I've got to read a book for Ronan. He just better not expect a book report on it because he certainly isn't getting one."

"I doubt whatever he'll expect from you, after you've read it, will be as simple as a book report," Kade said.

Amber thought of the picture in the front of the book. No, it wouldn't be that simple. Nothing was ever simple when it came to dragons. For a moment she wondered if she was doing the right thing coming back. It didn't take her long to know that she was. All she had to do was think about what the nine weeks and five days away from everyone had been like.

Crystal, who was the only other person at the table with them, said, "Don't forget you've got to talk to Rian first."

Amber grinned. "I do? It must have slipped my mind."

"What about?" Kade asked.

"Nothing," Crystal said quickly.

"I have to ask him a couple of questions about

several things Ronan said." She glanced towards Crystal. "Among other things."

"So when will you have time for me?"

Amber met Kade's gaze. "I'd like to say right now, but I've got a feeling things are going to get really crazy again."

"But I don't want crazy. At least not for another six months," Crystal wailed.

"Why six months?"

"Because then Flinn and Kade will have passed all their tests."

Amber frowned turning to Kade. "Didn't you have another test to do besides hold this place for a year?"

Kade nodded.

Crystal answered before he could. "Yeah, but we had someone attack us, trying to take our castle from us. As if we'd let anyone take Temolae Keep. We retaliated as a test."

"We would have retaliated anyway," Kade said.

"Yeah, but we used it as a test," Crystal said.

"Was anyone hurt?" Amber looked from one to the other as worry arrowed through her.

"No one died," Crystal said. "Well, no one that you know, anyway."

Why hadn't they told her they'd been attacked? That they'd needed to retaliate. They'd faced battle without her there to heal them. She shouldn't have wasted so much time staying away.

Kade reached for her hand, threading his fingers through hers. "We're fine. Stop worrying about it. There's always battles. Remember, we like to keep what's ours."

Amber smiled reluctantly. "And what's your neighbour's too."

Kade chuckled. "Yeah."

"A Gold just came into this room in the Void. It's that one that tried to kill you, Amber. The assassin we talked to at Ronan's," Crystal said to both of them.

"Daray, out of the Void now." Still holding onto Kade's hand, Amber turned to face him when he stepped out of the Void. "What do you want?"

"I'm on guard duty."

"No you're not. And stop watching me from the Void. I really dislike that." Amber pointed a finger at him. "Stay right there." She turned to Kade. "I'll see you later." Still holding his hand, her other one rested against his chest as she leaned in to kiss him. When she drew back, she held his gaze for a moment. *"I missed you."*

"Good. Remember that next time you think about taking off."

Amber grinned. *"I'm not going to take off again."*

With a glance towards her almost finished breakfast, she rose from the table, headed for the door. As she passed Daray, she said. "I'm serious. Stay here." She mentally searched for Rian, hurrying through the castle to corner him in a hallway. "I need to talk to you."

With a nod, Rian headed for the planning room, closing the door behind them. He sat at the table, across from her. "Welcome back."

Amber nodded. "Thanks."

"I was informed when you arrived last night, but I knew you would want to spend time with Kade. That is why I only told Crystal this morning."

"That's not what I want to talk to you about. First, what's the name of my second warrior?"

"Daray."

"He belongs to Ronan."

Rian grinned fleetingly. "Not since he talked to Doneele. His daughter has an extreme case of hero worship for you and Jasper."

"I thought he was going to stay out of her life."

"He was worried about her. I do not think he planned to talk to her, but she spotted him. Your brother took her to the theme parks on the Gold Coast as a reward for doing so well at school. Daray followed. Jasper said he could join them for the day."

"And this is okay?" When Rian nodded, she asked, "I mean, this won't cause problems?" Rian smiled. The same amused one his father used when she said something stupid. She glared at him. "Well?"

"It may cause problems, but having another loyal warrior at your back is never a bad idea."

She nodded, trying to think of a way to speak to him about Crystal.

"Was that all?"

"Not quite." She continued to stare at him, almost wishing he wasn't sitting there so patiently, waiting for her to speak. Why didn't he ask her what she wanted? "Crystal spoke to me this morning."

Rian continued to sit patiently.

Amber tried to wrack her brain for the right words. None came. "Oh come on, Rian, help me out here."

"She should not have bothered you."

"Yes, she should. We're friends. That's what friends are for. She wants me to tell you that if you like her, then there's no problem to the pair of you hooking up."

"And if I do not like her in that way?"

"Then tell her."

Rian remained quiet for several minutes. "Have you considered the problems it would cause you with Flinn?"

Amber stabbed a finger in his direction, leaning forward. "Don't you dare put this on me. If you're interested in Crystal don't you make me the reason you won't do anything."

"I am your first warrior. Your needs must come before mine."

"Well in that case, you're fired. Now go talk to Crystal."

Rian chuckled, rising to his feet. "I am not fired, but I will talk to Crystal." He paused. "Was that all?"

She thought of the book Ronan had given her. "Yeah. For now."

With a nod, Rian headed for the door, closing it softly behind him.

Amber rested her arms on the table, dropping her head on them as she breathed out heavily. "Damn dragons," she muttered, a smile tugging at the corners of her mouth. Before she could have Daray bring her the book she'd left on the table, Crystal spoke to her.

"Rian wants to talk to me. What's he going to say?"

"I wouldn't have a clue." She rose to her feet, heading for the door.

"But you must have some idea."

"No. Not really."

"Okay. I'm almost where he wants to meet me. I'll talk to you later."

Amber couldn't help smiling at the excitement that had been in Crystal's words. She hoped it worked out for her. Crystal would be devastated if Rian rejected her. She guessed she should have Daray bring the book to her. She hesitated. Surely she deserved at least a little break before she started. Mentally searching for Kade, she found him not far from where she was. Yep, she did deserve a break. She strode towards Kade's location.

Chapter Four

That afternoon, Amber lay on her bed, an arm flung over her eyes, the other stretched out so her fingers touched the book she'd just finished reading. The book she alternated between wishing she'd never opened and relieved that she'd been warned so they could prepare. Her head was filled with all the information she'd learned. It made her want to check on everyone. Even her grandparents. Obviously everyone could survive without her watching over them all the time. Even in battle. They'd managed to last nine weeks and five days without her protecting them.

She had no clue what she should be doing first. She needed to figure something out before she contacted Ronan. She wasn't going to let him call all the shots. He'd said they needed Dragon Mages, well they could start with her uncle. And if the Hell Hounds were definitely coming she wanted to make sure her mother could protect herself. An image of her mother with a gun at her head came to mind and she quickly pushed it away, not wanting to give into the fear and anger that image always brought.

And she'd insist that Ronan let her tell the mages closest to her how to store power. She didn't want all mages to know. That was plain crazy. Especially after what had happened with Shannon. She also needed more information. Knowing Ronan there were probably other things he hadn't told her and didn't plan to tell her. Reluctantly moving, she took out her phone and sent Ronan a message. *I'm ready to talk now.*

She noticed him come out of the Void in her planning room before he disappeared back into it. Rising to her feet, taking the book with her, she headed for the bedroom door, only to stop as Ronan came out of the Void in front of her.

"What have you done to the planning room?"

Amber shrugged. She had no idea what had been done since she'd been away. "You'll have to ask Rian."

"I can't stay in the Void in there."

Amber grinned. "Well that's handy." She mentally reached for Rian. *"When did you make it impossible for*

Golds to stay in the Void in the planning room? And can we do it to the rest of the castle?"

"The materials are hard to come by, which makes them very expensive. Only the planning room and Crystal's bedroom have been done. Golds can still enter those rooms from the Void, but they cannot stay in the Void while they are in them. You can also still communicate with your mind beyond the walls of those rooms."

Amber laughed. He knew her so well. Of course she wanted Crystal's room protected before hers. *"Thanks."*

"What did Rian say?" Ronan asked.

"That he's planning to do more rooms."

"Nice try, kitten. I know where the stone comes from and how impossible it is to get."

"Where does it come from?"

"In the Hell Hounds' world."

Amber stared at him with narrowed eyes. "You better not be saying that just to convince me to break the binding."

"No. It's the reason why places like Feralenzi, that were made centuries ago, are full of it and yet it's so rare now. There are two types. One that prevents anyone from walking through the Void and one that prevents mind talk outside of the area as well as Void walking. Obviously the second one is the more expensive." He gestured towards the book she held. "Have you read it?"

Amber nodded. Before she had a chance to say anything Ronan reached out and took her to the planning room, through the Void. "Would it hurt you to ask?"

"Probably." Ronan gestured towards a seat, sitting in one opposite. "Should we get all the questions, you've probably got, out of the way first?"

There was no way she was going to start with a question after that comment. "Actually I was thinking of starting with my demands." She sat down, placing the book in front of her on the table.

"This is for your benefit too. You don't get to make demands."

"Yeah, I do. My uncle will become a mage. My mother if she wants to be. And Crystal and Mum will learn how to store power. As well as anyone else one hundred percent loyal to me. None of that is negotiable."

Ronan stared at her, his gaze unblinking. Eventually he nodded. "I can see the benefits of those demands. Teaching Crystal and Donna about storing power would make our mages more powerful than anyone else's. Roger's from a powerful clan and it would be good to have them beholden to us. Giving your mother the means to protect herself, helps protect you. I'm impressed, kitten. A pity my sons never learned as quickly as you have."

"Maybe they would've learned quicker if they'd had a decent reason to."

"Are you saying surviving isn't a good enough reason?"

Amber smiled, trying to mimic Ronan's predatory one. "Surviving isn't as important as living. But then I'm human." She shrugged. "We tend to want to do more than just survive."

"Any more demands?"

"Not for now, but I'm sure I'll think of more later."

"Don't be smart, kitten."

"Does that mean your feeling of having missed me is wearing off?"

"You need to be taking this a little more seriously. It's been six years since the last binding was performed and already it's starting to fail. The binding before that lasted nine years. It's getting close to the point where it won't work at all."

"How do you know? Have you been working with them?" She remembered he'd once told her he was friends with some of his enemies.

"No, I listen and I hear rumours. It's not hard figuring out the facts when the same group wants to buy both a captive Gold and a Pliethin. No questions asked, no answers given. And the years are getting closer and closer together."

"Why couldn't you just follow one of them back to wherever they're taking the Gold and the Pliethin?" Amber gestured towards the book on the table. "Why did you need to get your grandfather's notes?"

"It was more than just the location. You've read them. Do you think you could have worked all that out by yourself? Without those details it would have been impossible to break the binding."

"I wasn't expecting you to work it out by yourself. I just thought that when you found their location, you could have got the information from them."

"They don't have this information. No one does but us. They're asking for pure Gold Warriors. That's what they think the problem is. Not that the binding is starting to fail, but that the quality of dragons they're using is causing the problem."

She didn't even bother suggesting they try and explain it was the binding failing. She doubted the Knights would be willing to listen. They'd probably think it was all about preventing the deaths of more dragons. "Can you get Pliethins to make more mages?"

"I'm already ahead of you, kitten. I have quite a few

stored away. We need the humans now. Once that would have been easy. They were gathered from the Knights."

"Why didn't all Knights become mages?"

"There used to be two types of mages. Dragon Mages created with dragon blood and a Pliethin and the Knight Mages created with dragon bone and a Pliethin. Both could see Hell Hounds, only Dragon Mages were able to use dragon powers. The Knight Mages gained more strength."

"I thought you didn't know how to make Dragon Mages."

"I didn't. It was in my grandfather's notes."

Amber gestured towards the book. "It wasn't in there."

"You don't have all his notes."

Why didn't that surprise her? "You have to stop doing this, Ronan. We aren't going to win if you keep half the information to yourself."

"We'll win." His predatory smile momentarily formed. "You'll make sure of it. Especially with the amount of lives at stake. Lives you want to protect."

"You don't want to see what will happen if any of those lives are harmed because you didn't give me all the information I needed," Amber said.

"You threatening me, kitten?"

"No." She held his gaze. "I'm warning you. Don't piss me off."

"Are you sure you won't have kids with Rian?"

"Positive." More so now that Crystal wanted him. But she certainly wasn't about to tell Ronan that. "What else do I need to know?"

"If I give you the rest of the notes, you'll want to share them."

"Probably."

"I'll think about it." He paused. "You need to find humans. More than the handful you've already decided you want to turn into mages. I have some, but nowhere near the amount we need. And don't go recruiting them from the same place they got Cooper from. That boy is useless."

She couldn't help smiling. Nor could she argue Ronan's statement. Cooper was almost afraid of his own shadow. "I have at least one other person in mind."

"You're going to need more than one. Who is it?"

"Angela."

"You better not be planning only to use teenagers as mages."

"You said you wanted mages we can trust. I trust Angela. She's also not weak like Cooper."

"Who else?"

Amber shrugged. "I've got a few ideas, but I need to talk to some people first."

"What ideas."

She smiled. "You've got your secrets, I guess I need a few of my own." She laughed when his eyes narrowed. "Don't worry about it, Ronan. I'll tell you all about it after I talk to a few people."

"Don't go making any mages without my approval."

She gave a half shrug, gesturing towards the book. "I also want to make copies of this so everyone else can read it. Without having to wait days for all of them to get through it."

"Only your immediate allies. Your people. Not your mother and grandparents though. Kade, Crystal, Jasper and Rian."

"What about Flinn? He should be able to read it too."

Ronan shook his head. "Sometimes you trust far too many people."

"Sometimes you don't trust enough. I will be letting Flinn read it."

Ronan rose to his feet. "Call me when you have some humans organised."

Amber also rose, nodding. "Of course I will." She grinned. "You've got the Pliethins we need." He disappeared into the Void and she mentally reached for Rian, asking him to join her in the planning room. Before she even thought about finding humans, she needed more copies of the journal.

Chapter Five

After Amber sent Rian to make photocopies of the book, she walked down a hallway beside Crystal, their arms linked together. When Crystal remained quiet, she asked, "I thought you said you wanted to talk to me."

"Did you give Daray permission to be in the Void?"

"No." Before Amber could tell Daray to get out of the Void, Crystal let go of her, reaching out her arm and disappearing. She stared at the spot her friend had been. It took her a moment before she could speak. "Daray, get out of the Void." He appeared, halfway down the hallway. Alone. Fear hit her. "Crystal?"

Crystal stepped out of the Void beside him. "What?"

"You were in the Void."

"No I wasn't. The moment I reached out for him he disappeared then reappeared further along the hallway. I'd nearly reached him when you called him out."

She stared at her friend, not sure if she should laugh at Crystal's disgruntled expression or try and convince her she'd entered the Void, without any help. "Uhm, Crystal, you disappeared."

The disgruntled expression was replaced by excitement. "Really?"

"Yes, really. Didn't it look any different to you? Didn't it feel harder to walk along the hallway?"

"No, I don't have that problem. When I'm in the Void, it's Flinn who slows me down. He can't move as quick as I can. The Void feels like walking around here. Just the very tiniest bit of haze over everything." Crystal grinned. "I can't believe I entered the Void on my own." Then she frowned. "I have no idea how I did it. Make your warrior go back into the Void."

When Daray looked at her, Amber nodded. He disappeared. She chuckled as Crystal muttered and stretched out her hand, dropped it again, paced back and forth a couple of times and then disappeared. "You're gone."

Crystal reappeared. "I am?"

"No, you're back again."

Crystal swore. "You might as well call Daray back out. I have no idea how I did that. I'll work on it later with Flinn. Anyway," she drew the word out, "Let's go to the fountain." She shot a glare towards Daray. "Since some people don't believe in giving a person any privacy."

"Would you like me to take you there?" Daray asked.

"You might as well make yourself useful," Crystal muttered.

Daray continued to look towards Amber, waiting for her to speak.

Amber barely managed to hold back a smile at the noise Crystal made when Daray ignored her comment. She nodded. "Take Crystal first."

"I was told not to leave you alone," Daray said.

Crystal glanced around the hallway. "There's no one else in the Void."

"Take Crystal. I'll be fine. You won't be long."

Daray reached for Crystal and disappeared, reappearing less than a minute later on his own. He held out his hand, waiting for Amber to take it before he took her through the Void to the fountain.

Crystal was sitting on the edge of the fountain, swinging one of her legs back and forth, the heel of her boot hitting the stonework of the fountain. "Now maybe we can talk. Without a million people listening in." She shot a look towards Daray.

Amber sat beside her, waiting until Daray had retreated several metres before she spoke. "What did Rian say?"

Crystal grinned. "Wouldn't you rather hear how good he can kiss?"

Amber laughed. "Sure."

Crystal threw her arms around Amber. "I can't believe he kissed me. Whatever you said to him convinced him to stop saying no to us."

"All I did was fire him."

"Are you sure?" Crystal drew away from her. "Seriously?"

Amber nodded. "Yeah, but he said he wasn't."

"That sounds like him." Crystal continued to grin. "I can't believe how happy I am. I seriously didn't think I could get any happier than I was. Absolutely nothing could steal my happy."

"Well…" Amber drew the word out.

"Oh please don't," Crystal begged.

"Should I start with the good news first?"

"There's good news?"

Amber nodded.

"Ronan's involved and there's good news?"

Amber laughed at the disbelief in Crystal's voice and in her expression. "Yeah. There's good news.

Although I don't think Ronan thought it was good news."

"That makes more sense. What is it?"

"We can tell Inge. And we can make her a mage if she wants."

"Inge? Our Inge. As in Angela, in Brisbane."

"Yep."

"Now?"

Amber laughed again. "No, not right now. Later."

"I can't wait. Do you know how hard it's been not to tell her? And she's annoyed with you that you didn't go to schoolies with us." Crystal paused. "What happens if she's not interested?"

"What do you mean?"

"Will Ronan do anything to her if she knows about dragons, but isn't interested in becoming a mage?"

"She's mine. It doesn't matter how Ronan feels about it."

"When are you going to tell me what's happening?"

"Tonight. I'm just waiting for Rian to get some photocopying done for me."

"Should I be worried?"

Amber stared at Crystal not sure what to tell her.

"I'll take that as a yes."

"Don't worry, I'll look out for you."

"How about I look out for you?"

Amber reached for Crystal's hand. "We'll look out for each other."

"Deal." She squeezed Amber's hand. "Now are you going to tell me why we're allowed to tell Inge about dragons?

Amber shook her head. "Nice try. You're going to have to wait until Rian comes back with the photocopies."

"That'll be ages away," Crystal grumbled.

"I doubt it. Not with how efficient Rian is."

"Well he better hurry up, because I'm dying to know."

Amber really wished Crystal hadn't used that exact phrase. She didn't want to think about anybody dying, let alone Crystal. "He'll be back soon enough and then you can read all about the latest surprise Ronan has for us. But I wouldn't look too closely at the pictures if I were you. They'll probably give you nightmares."

"That's just what I need," Crystal said dryly.

"We'll meet tomorrow morning and discuss it. All of us, including Jasper, Flinn and Rian. But no other warriors for now."

"Flinn isn't going to like that. If you get to have your first warrior there he'll want his," Crystal said.

"He won't be there as my first warrior. He'll be there as co-owner of Temolae Keep."

"He's still not going to like it."

Amber shrugged. "That's his problem." She wasn't about to tell Rian that he couldn't come to the meeting tomorrow because it'd upset Flinn. A lot of things upset Flinn. He'd just have to get over them.

* * *

Amber felt like closing her eyes and hitting her head against the table in the planning room. Why had she thought involving Flinn would be a good idea? All it was doing was ruining her morning. Instead of closing her eyes, she glared at him across the table. "I believe him." Out of everyone she'd given the book to, he'd been the only one who'd doubted the truth of what he'd read.

"You can't trust a single thing Ronan says." Flinn gestured towards the spiral bound pages in front of him. "This could all be part of a larger plan for him to become an Elder now he's on the Council. Look how he hid that he was Gold."

Explaining Ronan had only hidden that he was Gold until he finished making himself one wouldn't help. It'd only have others wanting to learn his secret. "He doesn't need to tell us all his business. Just like I'm sure you don't tell us all of yours."

"Can we return to the question no one has answered yet? Does anyone have suggestions of where we can recruit humans for Dragon Mages?" Rian asked.

"Humans are weak, useless creatures," Flinn said.

"We are not." Crystal glared at Flinn, then turned to Rian to nod slightly.

Amber fleetingly wondered what Rian said to Crystal. "Since no one seems to have any other ideas, I'm thinking of talking to a couple of Knights about it."

"You can't trust Knights," Flinn said.

"I've been told I can't trust you either."

"Who said that?" Flinn demanded.

Amber grinned "Ronan."

"You'd be an idiot to trust a Knight. I can't think of a single Knight that doesn't want to kill you, including your grandparents," Flinn said.

She refused to let his words bother her. "I guess I just tend to have that effect on people." She smiled, mimicking Ronan's predatory one. "How about you? Feeling murderous?"

"Don't torment him, Amber," Kade said directly to her.

"You're going to end up getting us all killed. I'm not about to let you involve my mage in a suicide mission," Flinn said.

"I'll do what I want," Crystal snapped.

Flinn glared at Crystal. "Shut up."

Crystal started to rise to her feet, but Rian, who was beside her, put a hand on her arm and she remained seated.

Flinn leapt to his feet. "Get your hand off my mage. I've already told you to stay away from her."

Amber rose to her feet, slamming her hands against the table. "You do not own Crystal. We told you that at the start."

"Then get me a mage I can own. One who'll do as they're told. One who knows their place," Flinn said.

As her frustration and anger increased, Amber had to force the panther from escaping. "You don't want a mage like that. You want someone who can fight with you. A mage who'll have your back and won't need to be told what to do all the time."

"A mage willing to be owned would be a weak human and you'd end up despising them," Jasper said.

"Better than one that'd get you killed by not following orders." Flinn remained standing.

Amber stayed on her feet too. "I've got other things to do today. Did you have any actual questions, or did you only want to argue?"

"I've got a question. How long have we got before all hell breaks loose?" Jasper grinned.

Amber reluctantly smiled, shaking her head. "I can't believe you went there."

Jasper continued to grin. "Someone had to."

Crystal giggled.

Amber's smile faded. "I have no idea. But I don't think we're going to have very long to get ready."

"That's what I thought." Jasper spoke directly to Amber, *"Do you want me to work with Flinn? I don't have a Gold."*

"No. Not for now anyway." Amber glanced around the table. "Any other questions?" She shot a look at her brother. "Real questions." When everyone shook their head, she straightened. "I'll let you all know when I have any news. I've got to organise a meeting with some Knights."

"You are not going on your own," Rian said.

"Of course not. I'll take Kade with me."

"And Daray."

Amber shook her head. "Only Kade. They'll be wary enough without me taking a heap of people with me."

Flinn pointed at her. "Don't forget, if you get yourself killed the deal with Ronan is over and you're putting Crystal in danger from him."

"I'm not planning to get myself killed. I've also got better things to do than sit around here listening to you complain. I need to ring a couple of people." She strode from the room, feeling Kade follow her. She'd ring Roy first and then Angela and Shylah. After that, she should probably have a talk to her mother. She had no idea how that conversation was going to go and guessed she should probably make sure Jasper was there too. And maybe her grandparents. She'd have to let them know about the Hell Hounds. Although she should probably keep the fact she was going to help Ronan break the binding, to herself. Some of the rest she'd tell them.

Chapter Six

It wasn't until that afternoon Amber, Crystal, Kade and Flinn were able to see Angela. They met her at her house, which they had all to themselves since her mother was still at work.

Telling Angela hadn't been as difficult as Amber had thought, but she'd been full of questions, including one in particular that Amber hadn't expected.

"And Flinn's not your boyfriend?" Angela asked Crystal again.

Crystal rolled her eyes. "I've already told you, it's Rian."

"I haven't agreed to that," Flinn said.

"But Flinn's never been your boyfriend. That's just something you made up to explain why you were hanging out with him so much and moved in with him," Angela said.

"This is probably why we stopped making Dragon Mages. You humans are irrational. They," Flinn gestured towards Amber and Crystal, "showed you what they can do. Kade turned into a dragon and all you can worry about is who Crystal's lover is."

"Slow down," Crystal said. "We've barely got together and at the speed you're moving our relationship along we'll be married with kids by the end of the month."

Flinn growled, sending a glare in Kade's direction when he chuckled.

Amber thought she better interrupt before a real argument started. "If you need some time to think-"

"Are you kidding me?" Angela grinned. "I so want to be able to do that." She gestured towards Amber's hands. "Show me again?"

When Flinn growled, Amber struggled to hold back a smile as she brought fire to her hands. "You might not be able to call fire."

"That's okay. Ice and lightning are pretty cool too."

"You do understand you'll be involved in life and death fights," Kade said.

Angela met his gaze. "From what you've said, pretty much everyone will be in danger once the Hell Hounds can come into our world again. No way am I going to sit back and let them get me." She grinned.

"After years of arguing with my mum about doing martial arts instead of ballet, it'll be good to know I picked the right activity. Sign me up."

"It won't be straight away. It might even take a week or two. We need to find other humans to recruit," Amber said. Last night when she'd rung her, Shylah had asked to have several humans, her father had brought into the clan, turned into mages. She still wasn't certain that was a good idea, but Shylah's clan would free Roger from his promise and let him see his human family if they could have extra mages.

"Yeah, we need ones that won't go to the dark side." Crystal grinned.

"You know, I might be able to help there. I can think of four people I train with who'd be perfect. I've also got a cousin who wouldn't freak and run for the hills at the first sign of trouble." Angela hesitated. "What about our families? When all this happens, how will we keep them safe?"

"I don't know. I guess we make sure we get to the hounds first," Amber said.

"Do I get to pick what bird I'll turn into?" Angela asked.

"What were you thinking of?" Amber asked.

"I love eagles."

"No way," Crystal said. "You want a bird that

can manoeuvre really good in battle. Stick with a goshawk. We got lucky with them. They're like the fighter pilots of the bird world."

The rest of the visit was taken up discussing various birds, and their abilities until Angela's mother returned from work. They left, promising to check out the people she suggested when she could get them all together. As soon as they were in a sheltered location, not far from Angela's home, they used the Void to return to Temolae Keep.

"What next?" Crystal asked.

Amber thought of her mother. Eventually she'd have to talk to her, but there were other people she needed to see first. "Kade and I will visit Roy and his family tomorrow."

"Why not tonight?"

"Roy's uncles wanted to be there."

"I hope you can trust them. I don't really know them," Crystal glanced towards Flinn, "but Knights are meant to be one of our enemies."

"It wasn't always like that," Amber said.

"It's been that way for centuries," Flinn said.

"Sometimes things change," Kade said.

Flinn met his gaze. "And sometimes the only change is that you die."

Crystal stepped between them, looking past Kade to Amber. "Let me know how it goes."

Amber nodded and watched as Crystal followed Flinn, leaving her and Kade alone. After a moment, she turned to Kade, reaching for him. "Am I doing the right thing talking to Roy and his family?" Only Amos had promised not to kill her. She was pretty certain Roy wouldn't and Isaac was fairly level headed, but Eliza… she wasn't certain about Eliza. Particularly since she was about to tell the woman that more danger was coming. Danger that could harm her son.

"Only time will tell."

That was what she was afraid of.

* * *

Kade brought Amber as close as possible to Roy's house. They came out at the park where they'd met last time and walked the short distance to his house. The front door opened before they reached it and Roy stood waiting for them. At his side hung his sword. Amber eyed the weapon. She hoped the fact he was armed wasn't an indication of anything. Like their intentions. Again she thought of how only

Amos couldn't attack her. The others had made no such promise. Maybe she should have made all of them promise before she'd healed Isaac. Then she would have only had to worry about Eliza.

Roy silently stepped back so they could enter, glancing up and down the road before he closed the door. "They're in the kitchen." He led the way.

Eliza and Isaac were sitting at a round kitchen table while Amos paced the floor. All were armed and Amber began to wonder if talking to the Knights was a good idea.

Amos stilled when they entered. "Just remember I'm the only one who can't kill you."

Amber grinned, trying not to think about how that fact had already occurred to her. Again. "Does that still bother you, Amos?"

"You're seriously not planning to stir him, are you Amber?" Kade directly asked her.

It wasn't stirring. She just wasn't about to let him think his words bothered her. She sat at the table placing several pieces of paper in front of her. They were photocopies of some of the hand drawn pictures of Hell Hounds from the journal Ronan had given her. "I've been told that an old enemy of the Knights and dragons will be returning to our world."

Amos picked up a picture. "Is this them?"

Kade sat beside Amber at the table. "Yes."

"Who gave you this information?"

Amber met Amos' gaze. "Ronan."

"What makes you think he's telling the truth?" Isaac took the picture from his brother, looking at it.

"Anyone could have drawn that." Amos gestured towards the page his brother held.

"It was drawn centuries ago by someone who'd seen them." When Amber finished telling them about the Hell Hounds, avoiding the parts where her and Ronan would destroy the binding, silence filled the kitchen.

It was Isaac who broke the silence. "How do you know when they'll come, and how do you know they are even coming?"

"We're going to have to tell them," Kade said directly to Amber.

She didn't agree. They were just as likely to side with the ones maintaining the binding. "Because the binding is failing. It hardly lasts at all now. It won't be long until it no longer works."

"Why should we trust Ronan?" Amos asked.

"He's one of the oldest dragons still living." She thought it best not to say he was the oldest dragon. No one knew that. "I trust his instincts of survival more than I trust his words."

"You said only mages can see these Hell Hounds when they're wearing someone else's skin," Eliza said.

Amber nodded.

"Then how are we meant to see them?" Eliza asked.

"You can't."

"Not without the help of mages," Kade said.

"Are you expecting us to become your allies?" Amos asked.

Amber shook her head. "Not exactly."

"Is it only humans that can become mages?" Eliza asked.

"You can't become mages, if that's what you're asking. Although have you thought about using your dragon abilities? Are any of you Gold? What about capturing a Pliethin?" Amber asked.

"We are Knights," Eliza stated.

"Think about it." Amber's gaze travelled from Eliza to Isaac. "What about the humans that you know."

"I can't expect any of my Knights to give up their humanity," Isaac said.

"How human are they when they consume dragon bone?" Kade asked

"That's different." Amos still remained on his feet, regularly pacing the kitchen floor.

Amber couldn't see how it was, but guessed arguing the point wasn't about to help the situation.

"Didn't you hear me, when I explained about Knight Mages? They have more strength, but most important of all, they'll be able to see Hell Hounds. They aren't mages, just stronger humans."

"I heard. I just don't know that we trust you enough to believe you," Isaac said.

Amber rose abruptly from the table, taking a step away, about to tell them if they didn't believe her she was wasting her time. Before she could speak there was a popping sound a bit like glass breaking and almost immediately a thud in the wall behind her. Her gaze was first drawn to the kitchen window she faced, focusing on the hole in the glass, before darting to the wall behind her. Directly behind where she'd been sitting a bullet was embedded in the wall. She mentally searched the area, her gaze darting around the room as she looked for safety.

Before anyone else could move, Kade grabbed hold of Amber, taking her through the Void, bringing them out in their bedroom at Temolae keep. Her phone began to ring. She ignored it. "Take me back. That was Wayne. I'm sure it was Wayne."

"Are you crazy?"

"No. We can't leave them there."

"They're nothing to us. They don't even believe

what we told them. I'm not letting you risk your life for them."

"Then bring them here. To the planning room." Amber's phone finished ringing, starting up again immediately.

Kade stared at her for a moment. "If they'll come."

"Try." She pulled out her phone and saw it was Roy. "Kade's coming to get you."

"Amos thinks you planned this."

Of course he would. "I think it's Wayne. I didn't have a chance to be certain before Kade took me out of there." She left the bedroom, running towards the planning room.

"Kade's here but they're arguing with him. We don't trust him."

"Go with him, Roy. I'm not about to get you killed after saving you twice."

"Is that what this is about? Because I owe you?"

"No, it's about surviving. We're not going to manage this if only a handful are willing to fight against the Hell Hounds. Go with Kade. If you go with him, your family will too."

"You better not get my family killed." Roy hung up and a moment later he appeared in front of her with Kade, who immediately disappeared back into the Void.

"Is everyone okay? Are you?" Amber eyed him up and down, not seeing any wounds and unable to smell blood.

"No one's hurt, but someone's still shooting at our house. The window broke before Amos dragged me out of the kitchen."

Kade stepped out of the Void with Eliza, his gaze meeting Amber's for a second before he disappeared again.

Eliza pointed a finger at Amber stepping close to her. "This is your fault. You brought this on us."

Amber pushed Eliza's hand away from her face. "No, this is the Knights' problem. That was Wayne out there."

Kade brought Amos out of the Void and left again.

"We didn't want to be brought here." Amos gestured towards his nephew. "You forced us to come here by kidnapping Roy."

Roy spoke before Amber had a chance to. "It was my choice to go with Kade. If we'd stayed there one of us would've ended up getting killed."

"Don't start sticking up for them, Roy. We're Knights. I won't have you siding with them," Amos said.

Chapter Seven

Kade stepped out of the Void with Isaac. "I think there's more than one firing at the house."

"Who's going to fix my house?" Eliza demanded.

Amber started to say it was Wayne's responsibility, but decided it was better to ignore the question rather than start an argument. "Did the Knights even try to find Wayne?"

"How do you know it was Wayne?" Isaac asked.

Amber glanced towards Kade, not quite sure what to say.

"She's a tracker," Kade said.

"Then why didn't you help us find Wayne?" Isaac asked.

About to make excuses, Amber stopped herself. "Why should I do your job for you?"

"Exactly. Why should we do your job for you?

Since when are the Hell Hounds our problem?" Amos demanded.

"Since humans are the Hell Hounds preferred prey," Kade said.

"Then why haven't we heard about them before?" Eliza asked.

The planning room door swung open and Rian stood there. "I was informed there were strangers in the planning room." Then he spoke directly to Amber. *"Are you okay? Unharmed?"*

"Wayne was waiting for me. We left when he started shooting at the house."

"We should return with warriors." Before Amber had a chance to agree with Rian, Isaac spoke.

"You can't take an army of dragons into a quiet suburb without drawing attention."

"He's probably gone by now," Kade said

"We could come out at the park and circle around," Amber said. "We don't have to take an army with us. Besides, we wouldn't be able to get an army there in a hurry. How many Golds would know the pathway to that exact location?"

"Ronan probably would," Rian said.

"If you're going back there, you're taking me too." Amos rested his hand on his sword.

Daray stepped out of the Void, holding a referdex that he placed on the table.

"What are you doing here?" Amber asked Daray.

"I sent for him." Rian crossed the room and opened the referdex, flicking through the first handful of pages at the front of the book. "What is the location you wish to go to?"

Amber gave him the address and moved closer to watch him find it. "I don't see how this will help," she said and then spoke directly to Rian. *"And don't even think about calling Ronan."*

With his finger on the location, Rian stepped back and gestured Daray forward.

Daray stared down at the referdex for a moment, then nodded. "I can take someone to this location through the Void."

"You're not leaving me behind," Amos said before he looked towards his brother, shaking his head. "You're High Protector of New South Wales. You can't be seen to be involved with dragons. You shouldn't even be here."

"Are we going?" Kade asked.

Amber nodded, her gaze still holding Amos'. She didn't really want to take him and would have preferred to take Rian, who she knew she could trust. Just because Amos couldn't harm her, that didn't make Kade safe around him. But leaving him behind wasn't about to convince him to help with the Hell Hounds. "Daray, bring Amos."

They came out at the park and Amber mentally searched the area for Wayne. "He's left. I'd say by car with the distance he's travelled. Jennifer and Stanley are with him."

"Impossible. Martin ordered him to remain at headquarters. The exit is under constant surveillance. There's no way he could leave headquarters without Martin knowing," Amos said.

"Then Martin must be involved." She wouldn't be surprised if he was. She didn't trust Martin at all.

"Why should I believe it was Wayne firing at us? Especially now that he's conveniently left the scene. Then you tell me Stanley was with him and expect me to trust you even when there's still no proof. Would you believe us, if we were the ones telling you?"

Amber stared at Amos. He was right. She wouldn't take his word either. Not without proof. "Okay. Let's track him down."

"Amber-"

She interrupted Kade, hearing from his tone of voice he was about to disagree with her. "We have to go after him now. While they're still together."

"You will take me with you," Amos said.

Amber nodded. "Of course." How else was she going to prove to him and his brother that the Knights were involved?

"If anything happens to me, my brother will hunt you down." Amos withdrew his phone holding Amber's gaze until she nodded. He turned away to use his phone, instantly turning back to her. "I can't reach my brother."

"I'll call Rian's phone. Your phones won't work in the dragons' world." She dialled the number.

"Then why do yours?" Amos asked.

Amber shrugged. "I have no idea. All I know is that they've been fixed so they can." Rian answered his phone. "Amos needs to talk to Isaac."

"I will put him on," Rian said.

Amber held out her phone to Amos, turning away from him once he took it.

"We can't go after them with so few people. We need more warriors," Kade said to Amber.

"We don't have time. And it's not like I'm planning to confront them. We just need to show Amos that they're working together. We can take care of them later."

Amos returned Amber's phone. "Let's go."

Amber searched around until she located Wayne and Stanley. If they didn't go after them soon, it'd be too late. They were nearly beyond the distance she could track them. Her tie to Wayne and Stanley wasn't as strong as it was to Kade and the rest of her people. Now she just had to figure out how to explain where they were. "A pity we didn't bring the referdex with us."

"I can go back and get it." Daray disappeared when Amber nodded at his suggestion, returning a moment later with the referdex.

Amber opened it to the page of their location trying to estimate how far away Wayne was. She turned several pages, pointing to a location she thought would be near him. "They're somewhere around here."

Kade and Daray tried to figure out a location close to that point they would both know. Amos paced nearby, his gaze continually searching their surroundings.

Amber wanted to tell them to hurry up. That soon it'd be too late. Maybe she should suggest that they spend some time learning the pathways through the Void a little better.

Kade closed the referdex. "Okay, we're ready."

Amber barely managed not to say 'finally' as she took Kade's hand. As soon as they came out of the Void she searched for Wayne and Stanley, quickly locating them. She looked in the referdex that Kade held open for her, pointing out another location. "About here." She waited impatiently for Kade and Daray to sort out the next destination, taking Kade's hand the moment he closed the referdex. She grinned as they came out in the shadows at the side of a building. "Come on. It's not far from here." She both sensed and heard the three of them follow her. She came to a stop at a street corner as the lights holding up the traffic changed and the cars started to move away. "Look, over there." She pointed to a vehicle moving away.

"We need to get closer. All I can see is four people in a vehicle, not who they are," Amos said.

"If we get too close, they'll see you. Do you really want them to see you with us?" Amber asked.

"I need to get close enough to confirm it's Wayne and Stanley."

Amber felt like growling. Then realised the panther was prowling restlessly and wanting to escape. She tried to calm down, pushing the panther away. "Fine." She flicked through the referdex as she mentally searched for Wayne and Stanley. She jabbed a finger at a page. "Here."

"Hurry it up." Amos glanced around, his gaze stopping on each passer-by that stared at him. "I didn't expect to be standing on a street corner this morning when I grabbed my sword."

"We can't leave from here anyway." Kade closed the book. He glanced around the street. "Over there." He pointed to a shadowy location between two buildings.

Amber ran towards it, Kade at her side, Amos and Daray following. Kade took her through the Void the moment they reached the shadows. Amber mentally searched for Wayne, frowning when she realised he'd changed direction. Looking at the referdex, she tried to figure out what location to head for next. Turning another page she stared at the map for a moment. "I think I know where they're headed."

Amos peered over her shoulder. "The headquarters."

Amber nodded.

Amos took the referdex, pointing to a location on the map. "Can you bring us out here?"

Kade shook his head, pointing to another location. "Here."

"No, that's too close. Where else?"

Amber again searched for Wayne and Stanley. They still seemed to be heading in the direction of the Knights' Brisbane Headquarters. Martin had to be involved. He wasn't a stupid man. If Stanley was leaving the headquarters he had to know about it. When Kade closed the book Amber looked over at him, taking the hand he held out. They went through the Void to arrive under a shady tree, some waist high shrubs growing along the footpath that they could hide behind.

"Where are they?" Amos drew out his phone, glancing down to touch the screen.

Amber pointed in the direction they'd come from. "They're only minutes away."

Amos crouched behind the shrubs holding his phone out, pointing it towards the road.

Amber joined him, taking out her own phone to record Wayne and Stanley together. She didn't have long to wait. The vehicle came towards them. Wayne driving, Stanley seated beside him. Jennifer sat in the back seat near a man Amber had never seen before. Then they were past them, continuing towards the headquarters. Amber rose to her feet, the others doing the same. She held Amos' gaze. It was close, but she managed not to say, 'I told you so'. "Do you know who was with them?"

Amos shook his head. "I've never seen him before."

"Are you ready to go home, Amber?"

She held up a hand in a gesture of wait to answer Kade. "Hang on." She kept track of Wayne and

Stanley until they disappeared inside the headquarters. "They all went inside the headquarters."

"Maybe Stanley was sent to bring Wayne back," Amos suggested.

"And just for fun they decide to drop by your sister's house on the chance we were there?" Amber asked.

"They had to have been watching the house," Kade said.

Amos was silent a moment, his expression closed. "Take me back to my brother."

Kade looked towards Amber. She nodded, taking his hand. When they came out into the planning room at Temolae Keep, Rian stood by the door while Eliza leaned against the wall across the room from him, glaring. Isaac and Roy were both seated at the table.

Silence filled the room and Amber looked at each of the Knights. "Say it out loud. Whatever you're talking about, don't leave us out of it."

Amos spun to face her. "Why? So we can tell you that Martin lied to us?"

Amber nearly took a step backwards from the anger in his voice. Instead she made herself step forward, holding his angry gaze. "Yes. If that's what happened, then yes."

"Amos." Isaac's voice was soft, but it was enough to have Amos taking a step away from Amber.

"He lied to all of us." Eliza pushed away from the wall. "He said Roy would be safe because Stanley wouldn't be able to leave the headquarters and they'd find Wayne. I want to know what's going on even more than you do." She stopped in front of Amber.

"What about the Hell Hounds?" Amber asked her.

"Right now I couldn't care less about the Hell Hounds. I want Stanley and Wayne taken care of. Stanley tried to kill my son. I don't care what Martin says anymore. He can't be trusted. Stanley needs to die before he can try and do it again."

Amber smiled. "I know exactly what you mean. And that's why I came to you about the Hell Hounds. I know what you're willing to do to protect your son. I'd do the same for my people. The Hell Hounds are coming. Vikki's last words were the hounds are coming. I didn't know what she meant at the time, but now I do. Wayne knows about them too. And maybe Martin. But it doesn't matter who knows. What's important is that we're ready for them. I want to go after Wayne and Stanley, but the Hell Hounds are the bigger threat."

"We'll think about it if Roy can stay here for a bit," Isaac said.

Eliza spun to face her brother. "No."

"Yes. Wayne and Stanley have no way of getting here. He'll be safe," Isaac said.

"There are other dangers here," Eliza said.

Isaac held his sister's gaze a moment longer before he met Amber's. "You came to us for help. Not the other way around."

She wasn't sure what he was getting at, but she didn't want him to think she owed him. "Not exactly. It was for your benefit I came to you. I didn't go to the trouble of saving Roy's life twice only to let him lose it when the Hell Hounds came."

"Why did you save his life?" Isaac asked.

"Because he's not my enemy." Ronan would have said it was because she was weak, but it was more than that. She had to believe it was more than that.

"So you did it out of the goodness of your heart." It was clear from Amos' tone that he didn't believe her.

"No."

"So it was calculated," Amos said.

"I wouldn't say that." Why couldn't he just drop it? She had no idea how to explain it.

"She did it because she's a healer," Kade said.

"Then if you're a healer, why did you try and kill my brother?" Amos demanded.

Amber grinned. "That was calculated. Even the healing."

Ronan stepped out of the Void. "What's going on?"

Amos and Eliza drew their swords. Isaac rose and Roy jumped to his feet a couple of seconds later.

"Why are they here?" Ronan nodded towards the Knights, his attention on Amber.

"Wayne attacked while I was visiting them."

"Did you kill him?"

Amber shook her head.

Kade spoke before she could. "He attacked from a distance, using guns."

Ronan turned to Rian. "You should have told me." Then he turned towards the Knights. "Put your weapons away. Surely I'm not that terrifying." He glanced towards Rian again, his expression hard, before he turned to Amber. "What exactly happened?"

Isaac spoke first. "This is Knights' business."

"It affects my mage. This is my business."

Amos gestured towards Kade. "Doesn't he claim she's his mage?"

Ronan smiled his predatory smile and Amber wondered if she should interrupt. Ronan spoke before she had a chance.

"Maybe he's mine too. Which would mean what is his, is also mine."

"Amber brought you here to protect you. She is not about to let harm come to you while you are enjoying her hospitality," Rian said.

"Sheath your swords," Isaac said.

Amos slid his sword into the scabbard hanging at his side. "This still isn't any of his business."

"I have arranged lunch. It is in the dining room," Rian said.

"Ever the peacekeeper," Ronan said softly. "War will come no matter what you do, boy."

Rian inclined his head, opening the door he still stood near.

"What makes you think we're going to eat any food you'll offer us," Eliza said.

Amber opened her mouth to tell Eliza she could starve for all she cared. Rian answered first.

"You have been offered protection for today. It is safe to eat the food."

Eliza glanced towards Isaac and narrowed her eyes, before looking away. "Let's get this over and done with then."

When Amber would have followed them, Ronan grabbed hold of her arm, tugging her to him. He waited until they had the room to themselves, closing the door on Kade who left after Amber nodded in reassurance. "Why did you bring them here?"

"I wasn't about to let them get killed."

"They are useless to us."

"They have humans that would be useful."

"But not loyal to us. I told you to find ones that'd be loyal to us."

"We also need ones who will fight the Hell Hounds regardless of their loyalty. How much stronger is a Knight Mage?"

"As strong as a dragon, or near enough that most can't tell the difference."

"Then what's the harm in making Knight Mages?"

Ronan stared at her, holding her gaze for long silent minutes. "We still need mages that are loyal to us."

"And we'll have some, but we also need people who will fight the Hell Hounds because they believe in protecting humans. That's what the Knights are about."

"So they say."

Amber smiled. Of course he wasn't about to trust anything anyone said. "Yep. So they say."

"You better hope this doesn't cause problems for us later." Ronan paused. "What happened with Wayne?"

"He nearly got me. He shot at me from a distance and if I hadn't moved, I'd probably be dead."

"You need to be more careful than that."

"What did you expect me to do? How was I supposed to know he'd do that?"

"Be more alert. Haven't you learned anything yet?"

Amber was tempted to say no, but she could see he was serious. "Of course I have."

"Then you should have been continually checking the area. With all of your senses."

"I'll do that in future."

"You're lucky there will be a future. Don't trust no one. Always expect someone to be waiting to stab you in the back and stay alert. It's the only way to survive."

"Even that might not help when we face the Hell Hounds." Images of the hand drawn pictures came to mind.

"It'll help."

"I want you to promise me that if anything does happen to me you'll protect my people."

"That wasn't our deal."

"Neither was this. Fighting Hell Hounds wasn't ever part of our deal. Only getting your lands back."

"Two. Name two and I'll protect them if anything happens to you in this war."

"Ten."

"Four."

"That's not enough. Ten isn't even enough."

"Four. Take it or leave it."

Amber stared at him for a moment, deciding he wasn't about to budge. "Kade, Jasper, Crystal and Rian."

"You think you have to ask me to protect my own son?"

Amber nodded.

Ronan threw back his head and laughed. "I have hope for you, kitten. I really do."

Some days hope was all she had. "I need to get to the dining room." Although Rian would probably prevent an argument far better than she could.

"Organise your mages by Saturday. They'll need time to train before our war begins."

"But that's only five days away."

"Then you better hurry." Ronan disappeared into the Void.

Amber glared at the spot where he'd been before she flung the door open and marched to the dining room.

Chapter Eight

The following morning Amber kept her eyes closed, seriously thinking about not getting out of bed. After she'd finally agreed to keep Roy at Temolae Keep yesterday afternoon, the Knights had returned to their own world, with some help from Daray. She'd thought the problems had been dealt with for the day. She'd been wrong. Shylah had rung wanting her to give approval for the humans they'd chosen. It had sounded simple, until she told Rian that she was going.

Shylah hadn't been impressed when she'd turned up with Kade, Rian, Daray, Crystal and Flinn. It had taken a lot of effort to convince Kade and Flinn, especially Flinn, not to take their warriors. Only the fact that if they had to leave the place in a hurry they had enough Golds to get everyone out immediately, convinced them. Once getting past that issue they'd then had to deal with Shylah's family wanting every human in their Castle to become a mage. Even Amber had known that wouldn't have been a good idea. They finally agreed to six. That included Roger.

They'd returned to Temolae Keep and Amber had thought that was the problems dealt with for the day, but Angela had rung. She'd wanted Amber to meet the humans she'd chosen. None of the people had known what was about to happen and had been expecting movies and pizza. Flinn had taken one look at all of them and had argued Angela's choices.

Flinn, Amber and Angela had retreated to the kitchen for a whispered argument. Kade, Crystal, Rian and Daray had remained in the lounge room with the rest of the gathering who were eating pizza and paying very little attention to the movie that was playing. Talking and laughing instead. It had taken them nearly half an hour to convince Flinn. Only Angela's warning that her mother would be home at ten seemed to help Flinn come to a decision quickly. Everyone was finally told the real reason they'd been gathered. Some had taken more convincing than others, but in the end all had wanted to become Dragon Mages.

Amber felt Kade stir on the bed beside her and she opened her eyes to see him change back into human form. She reached for him, not wanting to think about anything else for a while.

Crystal burst into the room. "Oops. Sorry."

With her arms still wrapped around Kade, Amber looked towards her friend, who didn't look at all sorry with how wide her grin was. "Sure you are."

"Flinn thinks we should hunt Wayne down. He said it'd be better to deal with one enemy at a time rather than wait and deal with them all at once."

Groaning, Amber rolled out of bed, reaching for her phone and weapons. "We need to find more humans. We've only got four days."

"How are we meant to do that?"

Amber shrugged as she tightened the sheaths at her wrists before strapping on her sword. "I haven't got a clue. It'd be so much easier if I knew what each person was really like."

"You can." Kade rose from the bed.

"How?"

"Read their minds."

"I'm not good enough at that."

"It sounds kind of wrong," Crystal said.

"I can help you," Kade said.

Amber stared at him a moment. "I suppose." Her words were hesitant.

"I still think it sounds wrong," Crystal said.

"Don't some jobs in your world expect you to have a psychological assessment before you can do them?" Kade asked.

"This is different," Crystal said. "You're going to invade their minds."

Amber met Crystal's gaze. "I don't like the idea of it, but what if we accidentally picked out some psychopath because we didn't know them?"

"You mean like Ronan?" Crystal asked.

Amber couldn't help smiling. "Yeah."

"I suppose, but it still feels wrong."

"Ask Flinn. I'm sure he'll tell you there's nothing wrong with it," Kade said.

"There's very little Flinn and I agree with so it's no point asking him. I'm sure we won't agree." Crystal turned towards Amber. "Do you need help with it?"

Amber shook her head, clearly hearing the plea in Crystal's tone for her to say no. "We'll be right."

Crystal grinned. "I'll let Flinn know that he's got time to help me with my Void walking. He always seems to find excuses to get out of helping me with it." Crystal left the room as quickly as she'd arrived, barely giving Amber time to say goodbye.

She stared at the closed door, wishing that Crystal hadn't pointed out how wrong reading someone's mind was. Not that she hadn't already had the thought herself, but it was worse coming from someone else.

Kade came to stand beside her, his own sword at his side. "Are you okay?"

"Yeah." She didn't have a choice. "How many do you think we'll need to find?"

"I don't know. You could ask Ronan."

That was the last way she wanted to start her morning. "Maybe after breakfast."

She was still reluctant to contact Ronan after breakfast and decided that it'd probably be best to check in with Rian before they went out for the day. Tracking him down, she found him teaching Roy in the training room. Daray stepped out of the Void less than a minute after she entered the room.

Rian moved away from Roy, sheathing his sword. "Take over for me."

Daray nodded, drawing his sword before crossing the room to face Roy.

Rian joined Amber by the doorway. "We will step into the hallway so we do not disturb them."

As soon as they were in the hallway, with the door to the training room closed, Amber asked, "Was there something you wanted to talk to me about?" She couldn't think of any other reason why he'd want to leave the training room.

"Ronan came to visit me this morning."

Amber wasn't sure she wanted to know what they'd talked about. Something that Rian couldn't say aloud couldn't be good.

"He wants me to become a Gold like him."

Yep, she'd been right. *"Why?"*

"I am sure he has more reasons than what he actually gave me."

"I'm sure he has too. What reasons did he give you?"

"That as a Gold he should have fathered at least one Gold by now. He does not want anyone questioning the fact he is Gold."

"Why you? Why not one of your brothers?"

Rian smiled fleetingly. *"I asked him that too. He said I have the greatest chance of surviving."* Rian remained silent for a moment. *"He told me of the deal you made. Why me? Of all the people you could have chosen, why me?"*

She really wished he hadn't asked her that. It wasn't a simple question or answer. She shrugged. *"What would you do if I died?"*

"Take revenge on whoever had killed you."

"You would?"

Rian nodded. *"Of course."*

"Is that because you're my first warrior?"

"It is one reason."

"And the other reasons?"

"Ask Kade what he would do if you died."

She stared at him a moment longer before she did as he asked. *"What would you do if I died?"*

"Where are you? Are you okay?" Kade asked.

"I'm fine. It was just a question Rian said I should ask you. What would you do?"

"I would avenge you," Kade said.

She started to protest, then remembered how she'd felt when she'd thought Vikki had killed him. *"I would do the same for you."* She could sense her own feelings reflected back at her from Kade. She held onto them for a moment, feeling almost like she could wrap them around herself. *"I have to finish talking to Rian. Then we can go to my world and find humans suitable to become mages."*

"I'll be ready," Kade said.

"I spoke to Kade. He basically said the same as you. But he loves me."

"We are dragons. It is expected of us. Not just for those we love. I owe you a life, but I would do it even without that. You would be worth avenging."

Amber felt slightly uncomfortable by his compliment. *"What would you do after that?"*

"I would protect the castle and your people."

"You would protect Crystal."

"Yes." Rian stared at her for a moment. *"This is your reason?"*

"I think I must be getting as complicated as your father."

"No one is that complicated."

Amber laughed, hearing the humour in Rian's thoughts. *"Maybe not."* She reached out and rested a hand on his shoulder. *"Crystal isn't the only reason. Just being Ronan's son puts you in danger. And not only from others, but also from your father and what he expects of you."*

"I would do all I could to protect you. But if for some reason you should not survive I will protect your people."

"Thank you."

"All of them. Not only four."

"Thank you." She let her arm fall to her side. *"I need to find more humans to turn into mages. I have absolutely no idea how many we'll need."*

"At least fifty. Preferably one hundred."

"You've got to be kidding me. How am I meant to find that many?"

"You will manage. You always do."

"How can you say that? I ran. Well, it was a walk, but I still left everyone."

"Everyone needs a break at some stage. You returned when it was time. None of us had to ask you to return."

What would have happened if she hadn't returned by now? If it had taken her a lot longer to figure everything out. She wondered if Ronan would have come up with a plan to make her want to return. She thought of everything that had happened Friday. From the late delivery to the man with the gun on her way home from work. Surely that would have been beyond even Ronan's planning abilities. Pushing that thought away, she started to say she'd better go, when another question occurred to her. *"Why are you training Roy?"*

"Because he is uncertain of Ronan, but he completely trusts you even though he keeps reminding himself he should not. If he is going to fight at your side he needs to be more efficient than he is."

"He told you that?"

"In a lot more words."

"Are you going to let your father turn you into a Gold?"

"It involves eating the heart of a Gold. He told me he already has a heart, frozen and segmented."

She wanted to protest, but as a Gold Rian would be able to protect Crystal a lot easier. *"It's your choice."*

She wanted to order him to become a Gold even though her mind shied away from the thought of anyone eating a dragon heart.

"If anyone was to find out I had eaten a heart I would risk becoming a renegade."

"It is your choice."

"I have the feeling you want me to say yes."

Amber smiled wryly. *"Crystal."*

Rian chuckled. *"Of course."*

Amber nodded. *"I need to go and find some more recruits."* When Rian nodded she started to walk away, searching for Kade. She found him in their room, removing his weapons. It was something she needed to do as well. She reluctantly removed her weapons, feeling half naked without them. She met Kade's gaze, holding it for a moment.

"Are you okay?"

She wasn't sure. This wasn't what she'd expected when she'd returned. But she would be. She'd come back for all of them. Come back to protect those she loved and keep them safe. Come back to be with them because without all of them she wasn't herself. "Yeah. Let's do this." She held out her hand, waiting for him to take it so they could travel through the Void.

Chapter Nine

By Thursday afternoon Amber still hadn't been able to bring herself to talk to her mother, but she was three recruits off reaching fifty. Her mother would bring her one person closer to her goal. If she agreed to become a mage. Amber dropped onto the edge of her bed, lying back, arms outstretched as she closed her eyes. "I didn't realise how many crazy people there are in the world."

Kade sat on the bed beside her. "I would have thought you'd have already known that. It's on your news all the time."

"Yeah, but that doesn't exactly seem real." She opened her eyes to stare up at him. "Like it all happens in a different world." Her phone rang and she groaned. "I really don't feel like talking to anyone." She glanced at the screen and groaned again. "Especially not Cooper."

"Ignore him. Call him back later."

She was tempted to, but guessed he'd probably keep ringing if she didn't answer. "Yeah?"

"I need you to visit me."

"Now? I've just got home, Cooper."

"You promised you'd visit me whenever I asked you to. I want you to keep the promise you made me."

She opened her mouth to argue. She'd never made him that promise. The only one he'd tried to get her to make was one to keep him safe. And she'd never actually made it.

"Please, Amber. Don't break your promise to me."

There was something in his voice that made her worry for him. Surely he was safe. "Cooper, are you absolutely certain I need to visit right now? Are you sure it can't wait until tomorrow."

"I need you to keep your promise."

She nearly swore, but was worried someone else might be listening. Who would be there with Cooper? Tahmid was dead and no one else should know where he was. "Okay, give me ten to get ready. I mean, it's not an emergency now, is it?"

There was a pause before Cooper answered. "Everything is the same as it always is. I just need to talk to you. Only you. In private. So don't bring anyone else. Okay?"

"Sure, Cooper. I'll get Kade to drop me in my room and then come back in an hour to pick me up." Amber rose from the bed, holding the phone with her shoulder as she pulled on her wrist sheaths.

"Can you make that three hours? I've got a lot to talk to you about."

"Three."

"Yes. Exactly."

Was that a message? Were there three people with him or was that how long they'd told him to tell her? "Is Elliot there? Or just you who needs to talk to me."

"Elliot's here too. We both need to talk to you."

"All right. I won't be too long."

"Ten minutes, right?"

"Yeah, see you then." She hung up, looking towards Kade who was now armed. She guessed he must have been listening to both sides of the conversation. "We have to save Cooper and Elliot."

"I'll organise Rian and Daray, you call Ronan. I don't know the paths to the inside of your place. Only outside. He'll probably be able to get you inside quicker."

Amber nodded, dialling his number as she strapped on her sword.

"You better not be ringing to tell me you need more time."

"Cooper and Elliot are in danger."

"Wait a minute." Ronan hung up.

Amber glared at the phone.

"Daray and Rian will be here in a minute," Kade said.

"Ronan just hung up on me."

Before Kade could speak, Ronan stepped out of the Void. "There's three of them. Wayne, Stanley and another man. In the lounge room. Cooper and Elliot are sitting beside each other on the couch. The men have guns. It was a lot better when Knights used swords."

"We have to get them," Amber said.

Daray stepped out of the Void with Rian.

Ronan pointed to Daray. "You will get Cooper." Then he pointed at Kade. "You get Elliot. Return them here and bring Rian back with you. I'll take Amber."

"They're expecting me to arrive in my room and for Kade to drop me off and leave straight away," Amber said.

"What is going on?" Rian asked.

"Wayne, Stanley and another man are holding Cooper and Elliot at gunpoint," Amber said.

"Wait until Amber opens the bedroom door before you grab the mages," Ronan said.

Kade and Daray nodded.

Amber reached for Kade's hand, momentarily linking her fingers through his. "Be careful."

"You too." His fingers tightened on hers before he let go, disappearing into the Void. Daray vanished too.

Ronan held out his hand. "Ready, kitten?"

She nodded.

"Try not to kill all of them."

"I hadn't planned to kill any of them."

Ronan laughed. "That's what you say now. Just remember not to kill all of them. I need to discuss some things with them."

She took his hand. As if she wanted to kill anyone else. "Fine." When they came out into her old bedroom, Amber let go of him, striding towards the door. Everything was quiet. A glance around her bedroom showed nothing out of the ordinary. Even Ronan was gone, hopefully in the Void, watching her. She hesitated, her hand on the knob as she searched the room on the other side of the door. Five people. All of them familiar except one. And even he was kind of familiar. He'd been with Wayne and Stanley when she'd tracked them on Monday.

When she swung the door open, all five men looked towards her. Amber had time to glimpse the bruises and blood on Cooper and Elliot before Kade and Daray stepped out of the Void and took them into it. Anger exploded in her and she knew why Ronan had warned her not to kill them.

"Drop your weapons and I won't hurt you." She couldn't promise the same for anyone else.

The other man laughed, pointing his gun at her. Amber jumped to the side as he fired. Kade, coming out of the Void with Rian, tackled the man. Daray attacked Stanley while Ronan stepped out of the Void in front of Wayne, grabbing his gun and tossing it across the room.

It was almost a disappointment. Her hands were curled into fists, anger filling her at the image of Cooper and Elliot that remained in her mind, and she hadn't managed to do anything more than give them a warning. "What made you think you could take on the dragons and win?"

"This is why they should die. If we let them keep breeding we'd be overrun and slaughtered," Wayne said.

"Most of you aren't worth the time it'd take to slaughter you," Ronan said.

"Why did you want me here?" Amber asked.

"We need a Gold," Wayne said. "We knew at least one would come after you."

"Shut up," the other man said.

"Daray, take them to my place and chain them up," Ronan said.

"He's my warrior, not yours," Amber said.

Ronan smiled. "And are you not mine?"

Her jaw clenched as she held back the words to argue that comment. "And are you not mine?"

Ronan chuckled. "It seems we have a bit of a dilemma then, kitten."

"Tell him he can house them and we will interrogate them," Rian told Amber.

"That's okay. You house them, we'll interrogate them," Amber said.

Ronan shot a look towards his son. "Stop interfering." He turned back to Amber. "Do you have somewhere secure?"

She nodded. "The dungeons."

Stanley struggled, trying to escape Daray. "You're not putting me in a dungeon."

Amber stepped close to him, eyes narrowing as she met his. "Does that worry you, Stanley? It should. Let me see if I can remember how it goes. Chained to a wall with no food or water until you talk. Isn't that right?"

"I should have killed you," Stanley spat.

"Yeah, you should have." Amber stepped away from Stanley before she faced Ronan again. "Well?"

Ronan nodded. "Have it your way. For now." His gaze slid past her to Rian. "You will be responsible for them. Make sure they're secure."

"Daray, take the Knights to the dungeons and lock them in separate cells," Rian said.

Daray nodded, disappearing with Stanley.

"You won't get away with this," Wayne warned. "You will pay for everything you've done."

"Shut up," the other man said.

"You shut up," Wayne snarled. "It wasn't you who lost a sister."

Before the man could reply, Daray returned, taking him into the Void.

"I don't see how you think you can make us pay," Amber said. "I'm not about to let you out of the dungeon."

"You think that'll stop them coming for me? They know where we are. They'll know who's to blame when we don't return. All you had to do was give us a Gold and none of this would have happened. You don't understand what we're protecting you from."

Amber waved Daray back when he stepped out of the Void and reached for Wayne. "Hell Hounds. But they're coming. No matter what you do, you won't be able to stop them."

"How did you find out? No one would have talked."

"You know nothing," Ronan said. "You Knights haven't got a clue."

"We are more than Knights. We're the inner circle. No other Knight is higher than us. The entire fate of the world rests on our shoulders."

"And you think killing dragons is going to protect the world? Then why is the binding still failing?" Amber asked.

"How do you know?" Wayne demanded.

Amber smiled, mimicking Ronan's predatory one. "We probably know more than you. The binding was never going to last forever."

"No, it's the Golds. They aren't pure enough."

"The last one you took was one of the purest Golds in existence," Ronan said.

"You don't know nothing," Wayne snarled.

"Really?" Ronan's predatory smile formed as he took a step closer to Wayne. "Ariana."

Wayne drew back as if struck. "No."

"You're going to lie to me?" Ronan demanded.

Wayne shook his head. "It can't be true. You don't know what they're like. It's nearly impossible to kill them. One got through during the last binding and he slaughtered eleven Knights before he was killed. Four of the ones who died were more than Knights. Stronger. Even they weren't enough."

"Just because you don't like something doesn't make it a lie," Ronan said.

Eleven Knights? Four of them Knight Mages? Amber began to wonder if she'd found enough humans to turn into mages. Maybe she needed to find more.

"She can't have been pure," Wayne said.

"She was from a long line of Golds. Everyone in her family is Gold. You can't get more pure a line than that. If her enemies hadn't handed her over to you no renegade would have provided so strong a line," Ronan said.

"The hounds are coming," Amber repeated Vikki's last words. "Even your sister knew."

Wayne struggled to escape. "I'm going to kill you for her."

"Better than you have tried and failed," Amber said. She couldn't afford to die. She had too many to live for.

"Take him away," Ronan said.

Daray took Wayne before Amber could protest. She turned on Ronan with a glare. "I wasn't finished."

"We'll get more out of him after he's been chained up for a while and realises he can't escape," Ronan said. "Go home."

"Not until Daray comes back for Rian."

"Go home. I've got better things to do than wait around here all day." Ronan grabbed hold of Rian and disappeared.

Amber crossed the short distance between her and Kade, reaching for him as she spoke. "Temolae Keep." The moment they came out of the Void, she searched for Rian. *"Are you okay?"*

"Yes. I will arrange extra guards for the dungeons."

"Amber?"

She met Kade's worried gaze and realised she still held onto him. She smiled. "I'm okay. I was just checking on Rian." She sighed. "I guess we should check Cooper and Elliot."

"I'll take you to them." Kade took her through the Void, bringing her out in one of the guest rooms where Cooper and Elliot argued together.

Chapter Ten

Elliot spun to face them, raising his hands. He dropped them before he could form a fireball. "They shot the Gold in front of us. They said we'd be next if you didn't come for us."

She hadn't even thought about that. Why hadn't she asked about the Gold that had been guarding them? Guilt hit her and she forced it away. She had to focus. "Where is he?"

"They dumped him in Cooper's room." Elliot rubbed at some of the dried blood on his face. "I was standing right next to him when they shot him."

Amber reached for Elliot, who was closest to her, planning to heal him.

Elliot jerked away. "Don't go messing with my head. I don't want to end up like Miles."

"I didn't do anything to Miles."

"The dragons did. He told me they used to put their hands on him and mess with his head."

"He didn't tell me anything like that," Cooper said.

"I knew him. Before they took us, I knew him," Elliot said.

"When did he tell you this?" Amber asked.

"It was before you caught him. That's part of why I went with you. I knew it was only a matter of time before they started messing with my head too. I didn't know he'd lost his mind. Not until Cooper told me. I don't want to end up like that."

Amber stared at him for a moment. She'd never even considered that she might be able to heal Miles. Hadn't thought that something might be physically damaged inside his head. "I was only going to heal what Wayne did to you. I'm not a dragon. I'm a mage."

"She'd never hurt us," Cooper said.

Elliot shrugged. "Maybe not, but I'm not about to risk it."

"I can't make you let me heal you." She smiled when Elliot snorted in disbelief. "Okay, maybe I could make you, but I won't force you." She turned to Cooper. "Can I heal you?"

"Yeah. I trust you." Cooper stepped forward.

Placing her hands on him, she searched for the

dragon blood in him, healing him before she let her hands fall back to her sides. She looked from one to the other. "Do you want me to turn you into proper mages? Ones that can become birds."

"I don't know," Cooper said.

"Would we be expected to fight?" Elliot asked.

"No, but you'd hopefully be able to protect yourselves a bit better."

"I'll think about it," Elliot said.

"You only have until Saturday. That's when the next mages are to be made."

"I will," Cooper said. "I'll become a proper mage and I'll," he swallowed visibly. "I'll fight at your side."

"You don't have to," Amber said.

"You came."

Amber nodded. "You were in danger."

"I felt so useless. I know I can't fight. And I probably won't be able to fight very well even by becoming a proper mage, but I'm sick of being weak. I thought I could hide. But we can't, can we?"

Amber shook her head. "Not if we want to be safe."

"Fighting won't make you safe," Elliot said.

"Protecting yourself will make you safer than if you run," Kade said.

"I'm sick of being scared all the time." Cooper

glanced at Elliot before he returned his gaze to Amber. "Every minute of every day."

"You'll always be scared," Elliot said.

"And you're not?" Amber stepped closer to Elliot. "I smelt it on you. When I reached out to heal you, I smelt fear. So leave Cooper alone."

Elliot stared at her. "Why?"

"I don't get what you're asking."

Elliot gestured towards Cooper. "Why protect him? He's nothing to you."

She tried to figure out how to answer him. Why did everyone have to keep asking her questions? "He's my friend." She felt Cooper move close to her shoulder.

"And I'm not?"

Her gaze was drawn to the bruises and broken skin visible on him. "You aren't interested in being my friend. You won't even let me heal you. Friends trust each other."

Elliot laughed, a sharp, bitter sound. "Like I'm about to trust anyone. I can't even trust what I've believed all my life. None of this should be real."

She knew how he felt. Had struggled to accept the reality of it herself and still often wondered at her own sanity. "But it is. With worse to come."

Elliot held her gaze a moment before he squared his shoulders. "Heal me."

Amber nodded, reaching for him, resting the palm of her right hand against his cheek. It didn't take long to find the dragon blood in him and she watched as the marks faded from him, only the dried blood left behind. "You don't have to stay here if you don't want to." She drew her hand away.

"Where else would I go?"

"Anywhere. I'd find somewhere for you."

"You said worse is coming. Is there anywhere that will be safe from it?"

She shook her head.

"Then why tell me I can leave? Why let me go somewhere that isn't safe?"

"Because nowhere will be safe. Even here won't be safe."

"Dragon lands will be fairly safe from the Hell Hounds. They've always struggled to enter our lands, but that won't make our lands safe. Survival of the fittest has never been about safety," Kade said to Elliot.

"I'll stay. I just can't promise I'll fight. Or is that what you're expecting me to do if I stay?" Elliot asked.

Amber shook her head. "No. But if you're not

going to fight, just don't get in the way when we need to." She held his gaze until he nodded.

"Are you going to tell us about the Hell Hounds?" Cooper asked, still at her shoulder.

Amber faced him. "I'll get Rian to tell you. I've got other things to do tonight." Things she'd been putting off.

"Okay."

Amber stretched out her hand towards Kade. *"Take us to our room, please."*

He crossed the space between them, holding her hand and instantly taking them through the Void, coming out into their room. "What things?"

"I need to ring Mum." She dreaded it more than she'd dreaded stepping into the lounge room earlier, knowing she was about to face three Knights with guns. There was definitely something seriously wrong with her.

"You could leave it until tomorrow," Kade said.

She shook her head. "No. I've put it off every day. She'll probably want some time to think about it."

"I'll go with you." He continued to hold her hand.

"Good." She grinned. "Just in case I need a quick escape." She held onto his hand a moment longer before she let it go to sit on the edge of the bed, pulling out her phone. She stared at it a moment then decided she should probably let Rian know that Cooper and Elliot needed to be told about the Hell Hounds. Even after she mentally contacted him, she continued to sit there.

Kade sat beside her. "You could tell her you want to see her tomorrow. Just because you ring her now doesn't mean you have to see her tonight."

She thought about it. Almost agreed, then shook her head. "No, it's probably better to get it over and done with." Taking a deep and not so calming breath she dialled her mother's number.

"I don't hear from you for ages and when you do ring, it's during dinner," Donna complained.

Maybe Kade was right. She probably could leave it until tomorrow. What was one night? An image of a gun at her mother's head came to mind. "I wanted to talk to you."

"Can it wait until after dinner? Can't you ring me back then?"

She guessed it could wait that long. And she should probably eat too. Although letting herself get hungry wasn't as big a problem for the panther as it used to be. Not now she had more control over it, but it still wasn't a good idea. "I need to see you in person. Where are you?"

"In Brisbane. At my parents' house."

"What? They have a house in Brisbane? Since when?"

"They've owned it for decades. Even before I was born."

"Then why didn't Grandma stay there? Why move?"

"If you're just planning on arguing with your grandparents you can wait until I leave to see me."

She wasn't planning to, but there was a good chance it would happen anyway. "How long will you be there?"

"We're staying the weekend."

"We?"

"Gary, Miles and myself."

Amber rose to her feet, starting to pace the floor. "You should have told me."

"I don't need to get your permission to do things, Amber. How about we drive up to the coast tomorrow and see you?"

"I'm not there. I'm with Kade."

"When did you get back with him?"

She hesitated. "Friday."

"Nearly a week ago."

"Yeah."

"So I'm meant to tell you things and you don't have to tell me anything."

She winced at the anger in her mother's voice. Maybe she should have rung her earlier. "I need to talk to you."

"What about?"

She started to tell her mother, but decided to use the easiest topic instead. "Miles."

"I should have known. It's always about everyone else."

"You and Gary too."

"Don't even think about it."

Amber halted in her pacing. Did her mother know? "Think about what?" Her words were cautious.

"I'm not getting back with your father. He's only interested because his girlfriend is dead."

She shook her head, trying to make sense of the conversation. Maybe she could put the discussion off one more day. No, then she was sure to find yet another excuse not to see her mother. "Where are you?"

"I already told you. At my parents' place."

Amber gritted her teeth, holding back the sarcastic comment that immediately came to mind. "I need an address."

"Why? You're not coming here to cause problems. I'll meet you somewhere tomorrow."

She took another deep breath. It helped calm her as much as the earlier one had. "Either tell me or I'll track you down myself and I'm likely to be really pissed off by the time I get there."

"Don't talk to me like that, Amber. I'm still your mother even if you think you're some great warrior who has to save the world."

"Oh forget it. I was probably wasting my time even thinking about asking you." She hung up, tossing her phone onto the bed before she started to pace again.

Kade stepped in front of her. "Rian's organised dinner for us. Want me to take you to the dining room?"

"Is anyone else there?"

Kade shook his head.

"Okay."

"Do you want to get your phone first?"

"No," she muttered, glancing towards the bed.

Chuckling, Kade grabbed her phone before he took them through the Void to the dining room. He placed the phone on the table near her plate.

"I didn't need it." She dropped into her seat, staring at the phone. It wasn't like she'd left it that long to tell her mother she'd returned. It wasn't even a week.

"Are you going to eat?" Kade sat beside her, picking up his cutlery.

"Yeah." She sighed. "Why couldn't things have stayed quiet for at least a couple of days? Why'd they have to go crazy the moment I returned?" She picked up a fork, pushing the roasted vegetables around on her plate. "Even a day. Surely one day of peace wasn't too much to ask."

"It would have been nice. Especially after how long you were gone." Kade reached out to draw her closer, his arm staying at her waist as his head rested on hers. "We've got tonight to ourselves now."

"Yeah. I–" Her phone, beeping a message, cut her sentence short.

"Don't look at it," Kade said. "I should have listened and left it in our room."

She tried to ignore it. Tried to eat her dinner. But her gaze kept being drawn back to her phone. In the end she gave up and checked the message.

"It's from your mother, isn't it?"

Amber nodded. "She sent the address."

"When are we going?"

"I haven't decided if I will yet." She was still annoyed.

Kade raised his eyebrow. "Really?"

"Okay. Fine. We're going. But not until after dinner. She can wait."

Chapter Eleven

They didn't leave straight after dinner. Rian came to tell them that Ronan had arrived to question their prisoners.

"Try not to let him hurt them," Amber said to Rian.

Kade shared a look with Rian before he turned back to Amber. "It's an interrogation, Amber."

"Yes but–"

Rian interrupted her. "I will tell him he is not to kill them."

She wanted to argue his words, but doubted he'd be able to make Ronan listen anyway. "Fine. I'm going to see my mum."

"Where will you be?"

Amber pulled up the message on her phone and read off the address. "I'm not sure how long I'll be. She's at my grandparents' place."

"Take Daray with you," Rian said.

"No. I'll be fine."

Rian stared at her a moment. *"I will be telling Ronan yes. I am your first warrior. I should not have been left behind today. I should have been in the Void watching over you."*

"Don't do this for me. Only do it because you want to."

Rian grinned fleetingly. *"Does it count that I want to do it for you? And for Crystal."*

Amber shrugged. *"I wouldn't have a clue."*

"It must remain a secret. You, Kade and Crystal are the only ones Ronan will allow me to tell. Everyone else is to believe that I hid what I was, like Ronan did. Not even my mother or brothers are to know. Everyone will think that first Ronan helped me hide what I am, then I continued to."

"Why won't he let your brothers know?"

"In case they are jealous that he chose me over them."

"Are they likely to be?"

Rian shrugged. *"Anything is possible."* He looked towards Kade, drawing him into the conversation. *"I will tell you when I tell Crystal. I will inform Ronan he is not to kill the prisoners."* When Amber nodded, Rian headed for the door.

Kade waited until Rian had left before he held out his hand. "Ready to go?"

"No, but I guess we should."

"You want to remove any of your weapons first?"

"Not bloody likely. We're going to my grandparents' home."

Kade chuckled as he took her hand. "I can't get us straight there, so are you sure you don't want to disarm?"

She hesitated. "I'll leave my sword behind and wear long sleeves to hide my wrist sheaths. I'm not about to walk in there unarmed."

Kade took them first to their room where they left their swords, and Kade slid a knife into his boot, while Amber pulled on a long sleeve shirt over her dragon-leather vest. Then he took them to a narrow grassed laneway between two houses, an unpainted timber fence bordering it. A taxi was waiting around the corner for them.

"When did you organise this?" Amber gestured towards the taxi.

"I got Maira to organise it as soon as you decided we were going."

Amber turned to glare at Daray as he came around the corner after them. Obviously Rian had ignored her when she'd said she didn't need Daray. And Kade must have known he was coming since Daray knew exactly where they'd be. She sat silently in the back of the taxi, between Kade and Daray. She had no idea what she was going to say to her mother. She'd even forgotten that she was going to ask her brother to be there with her. Quickly sending him a message, she waited for his reply.

It arrived just as the taxi pulled up in front of her grandparents' house. She hopped out and stared at the brick and wrought iron gates that rose in front of her, an imposing brick house set well back behind them. This was her grandparents' house? When Daray came to stand beside her she turned to him. "Can you collect Jasper? He's at home."

With a nod, Daray strolled away. As soon as he was hidden by the shadows he entered the Void. Amber wasn't certain if she should wait for Daray to return with Jasper, or go inside.

Kade joined her on the footpath. "Are we going in?"

"Maybe."

"They probably already know we're here. See the camera?"

Great. That was just what she needed. Striding forward she found that the gate was locked. *"How are we meant to get in?"*

"Probably by asking. But I don't think you want to do that." With a grin, Kade held out his hand.

Wondering what he planned to do, she took it. They entered the Void and Kade dragged her through the fence. She felt a moment of pain then they were on the other side, pushing their way through the Void towards the front door.

Kade pressed his hand against the door. "They've done something to prevent us from staying in the Void inside the house. Or at least entering while in the Void."

"All right, let's do this." The moment they were out of the Void she let go of his hand, knocking on the door. Before the door could be opened, Jasper and Daray stepped out of the Void beside her. She guessed Daray had also tried to walk through the Void and into the house.

"*Who's in there?*" Jasper asked.

Amber shrugged. "*I haven't got a clue. We're going in there blind.*"

"*Not exactly what I wanted to hear,*" Jasper said.

The door swung open and her grandfather stood there. From the look of it, she guessed he wasn't happy to see her. He was probably going to be even more unhappy once he found out why she was there. "I need to see my mum."

"Why? To upset her some more?"

'None of your business' probably wasn't going to

get her through the door. "If she didn't want to see me, she wouldn't have given me your address."

"We actually need to see all of you," Jasper said.

"Why?" Charles demanded.

"We want to talk to everyone at the same time," Jasper said.

Charles stared at him for several minutes, and Amber had begun to think he'd say no, when he stepped out of the doorway so they could enter. He stepped back into the doorway once Jasper and Amber were inside.

"You're not going to leave my friends outside," Amber said.

"I'm not about to have dragons in my house," Charles said.

Amber started to argue, but Jasper interrupted. "Then I guess we won't be sharing any information with you. That'll make Ronan happy. He didn't want us to tell you."

Amber almost laughed at her grandfather's expression. "Tell Mum I'll talk to her tomorrow. I'll meet her somewhere away from here."

Charles pointed at Jasper. "You better not be lying." When Jasper shook his head, Charles stepped aside and let Kade and Daray in. "Try anything and I will kill you. Both of you."

Kade glanced towards Amber. *"Looks like your family are as happy as ever to see me."*

She tried not to laugh and only succeeded in making a slightly strangled sound. The smile she couldn't hold back, especially when her grandfather glared at her.

"I can throw you out just as easily as I let you in," Charles warned.

Amber mentally searched the area, thinking he might have other Knights visiting to be able to speak that statement like he believed it was possible. She couldn't find anyone. Not even her mother. It was like being in the Knights' headquarters. She tried to search beyond the house. It was impossible now the front door was closed. "Where's my mum?" While she waited for Charles to answer, she spoke directly to her companions. *"This place is built out of the same stuff the Knights' headquarters is made from."*

"What I want to know, is how he got this house so quickly," Jasper said.

"Mum said they've had it for decades. I guess this is their house from when they lived in Brisbane. Back when Grandad was the High Protector," Amber said.

Charles gestured towards the closed door on the far side of the entryway. "Through there."

Amber led the way, opening the door to find another corridor. "Where?"

"Third door on the left."

She hurried along the hallway, sensing everyone following behind her. When she reached the door she cracked it open, mentally searching the room before she swung it open. Seated around a table was her mother, Gary, Miles and Helen. Everyone except for Miles turned in her direction.

Donna rose, heading towards Jasper. "Your sister didn't tell me you were coming." She hugged him, kissing his cheek.

Jasper smiled. "It was a last minute decision. But aren't you glad to see me?"

"Of course I am." She tugged him towards the table. "Come and sit down. Have you had dinner?"

Jasper sat next to Helen. "I'm fine. We're not here to eat. We've got some information to share with you."

Amber crossed the room to the table, Daray and Kade on either side of her. She sat down, Kade beside her. Daray remained standing behind her. "We've got two things to talk to you about."

It didn't take Amber long to wish she'd waited to talk to her mother alone. Charles and Helen constantly interrupted with questions, arguments and demands. When Amber asked her mother if she wanted to become a Dragon Mage there were only arguments. Even Jasper couldn't calm Charles and Helen.

When Charles rose to his feet to glare across the table and yell some more, Amber rose too. "Would you rather someone kill her? As long as I'm a mage, she's at risk too. And we've already figured out that the only way I can stop being a mage is if someone kills me."

"Will you stop talking about killing all the time?" Donna asked.

"I wasn't. I was talking about dying," Amber said.

"Killing, dying, all of it. Just stop." Donna brushed Gary's hand away when he reached for her.

"I'm trying to keep you safe," Amber said.

"That's not your responsibility." Donna looked from Amber to Jasper and back again. "Don't either of you understand? That's my job, not yours."

Amber slammed her hands against the table, wishing she hadn't when she recalled her grandfather had done the same earlier. "Then become a mage. Take the responsibility and become a mage."

Donna rose from her seat, holding Amber's gaze. "Why? So I can become a killer like my children?"

Amber's jaw dropped as she continued to stare at

her mother. She took a step back, her mouth closing. "Is that how you see us? As killers?"

Gary rose to his feet. "Your mother doesn't mean that, she's just upset. Finding out you'll have to face something worse than dragons-"

Amber interrupted Gary as Helen, Kade and Jasper stood up, leaving only Miles seated. "There's nothing wrong with dragons. Or at least not all dragons."

"Of course there's something wrong with dragons," Charles said.

Amber opened her mouth to argue with him then snapped it closed. There was no point. She was obviously wasting her time. "The lot of you can get killed. See if I care."

"You obviously do care."

Amber ignored Gary's words, his soothing tone annoying her. She pointed a finger at Charles. "I didn't have to warn you. I don't know you, I don't want to know you and I don't care about you." She gestured towards Helen and Donna. "I came here for them. And as much of a bitch as Grandma is, she's still my family."

"Amber! Apologise immediately," Donna ordered.

"Oh, like you haven't said the same before," Amber said.

"We are not discussing my behaviour right now. We're discussing yours."

Amber shook her head, staring at her mother. "Unbelievable. I came here to warn you. To save your lives. And what do you do? Forget it." She turned away. "Just forget it."

"Amber–" Jasper began.

"Forget it. I'm out of here." She strode towards the door, sensing Kade and Daray following.

"Amber." Jasper ran after her, grabbing her arm before she could step out of the room.

Amber shook him off. "I'm going home, Jay. Do you want Daray to take you home?"

"Don't go like this, Amber."

"Let her go," Charles said. "Running away seems to be all she knows how to do."

"I'm not running away. You know my number if you're interested. I'm just not sticking around here to waste my breath arguing." She held her grandfather's gaze a moment longer before she started to turn away.

Chapter Twelve

"What about Miles?" Kade asked Amber directly.

She looked towards Daray. "Take Miles back to Temolae Keep for me."

Donna hurried towards Miles' side, holding onto his upper arm. He didn't even look at her. "You're not taking him back just because you're angry."

"I'm not angry. I'm disappointed. Isn't that what you tell me? And Miles has nothing to do with it. I was given some information that might help fix him." Amber remained in the doorway. "Or don't you want him fixed?"

Donna continued to hold onto Miles' arm. "What sort of information?"

Amber shook her head at the suspicion she heard in her mother's voice. "This just keeps getting better and better," she muttered.

Gary moved close enough to Donna to place a

hand on her shoulder. "Let him go. We've done everything we can. Nothing has helped. Let him go."

Tears pooled in Donna's eyes as she slowly let go of Miles. "He doesn't like the dark. You have to leave a light on for him."

Amber nodded, holding her mother's gaze a moment longer before she nodded towards Daray who was within arms' reach of Miles. He took hold of Miles' arm, leading him from the room. Amber guessed he couldn't use the Void from her grandparents' house. "I'll send Daray back for you, Jay."

Jasper nodded. "Give me an hour. I'll talk to them."

Amber turned away again, ignoring her grandmother telling her mother to quit snivelling and stop being so weak. She'd barely taken a step when her phone rang. Taking it from her pocket she saw it was Rian. "Yeah."

"We are under attack. Knight Mages in the dungeons."

Just what she needed. Instead of fear or worry, weariness hit her. How had she reached this point? She tried to dredge up some fear. It didn't seem right not to have at least a little. "How did they get in there?"

"We need you back immediately. They have already rescued one prisoner."

"Okay." Returning her phone to her pocket, Amber turned to Kade, taking the hand he held out to her.

"We can't leave through the Void from here," Kade said.

Nodding, Amber broke into a run.

"What's happening?" Jasper chased after them.

"We're under attack. Knight Mages." Amber flung the front door open.

Charles followed. "Get back here and explain yourself."

"Send Daray back for me," Jasper said. "It's my castle too."

Amber nodded, then tightened her grip on Kade, meeting his gaze as they stepped outside. He took her through the Void, bringing them out in their room where they grabbed their swords. As soon as she'd buckled hers on, and removed her long sleeved shirt, Amber took Kade's hand again. He brought them out in the dungeons, stepping away from her to draw his sword, attacking the Knight Mage that came for them.

Amber mentally searched the area, finding Crystal and Flinn already there. Daray was fighting nearby and she ordered him to fetch Jasper. Stanley and Wayne were in separate cells and the majority of the Knight Mages seemed to be around Wayne. And for some reason, she could sense numerous Pliethins. "This way," she said to Kade. "They're trying to rescue Wayne."

She raced through the fighting, coming into Wayne's cell in time to see them unchain him. She launched a fireball at him. One of the Knight Mages grabbed hold of Wayne's arm and pushed their fingers into the wooden cage hanging at their neck on a chain. Dodging a blade, she tried to reach Wayne in time, turning into a goshawk to fly through the crowd. As she landed in front of him, becoming human, reaching out to grab hold of him, he disappeared with the Knight Mage holding onto him. All around them they began to disappear, touching their fingers to the wooden cages they wore. Amber felt Ronan come out of the Void nearby as she threw herself at a nearby Knight Mage, grabbing at the chain his cage hung from.

The chain broke and the man stumbled away from her. Another Knight Mage grabbed his arm and disappeared into the Void with him. She swore, glancing down at the chain wrapped around her fingers. It was all they had of the Knight Mages. They'd all disappeared.

Ronan strode into the cell. "How could you let them get away?"

Amber held up the wooden cage. It dangled from the chain. A Pliethin glowed inside the seven centimetre square cage. "They used these. Why didn't you tell us they could use these?"

"I didn't know. There was nothing about it in my grandfather's books." He glanced around at the warriors in the cell with them. "Get out. All of you, out."

Kade, who was in the doorway, stepped into the cell, gesturing for the warriors to exit. "We've still got Stanley."

"And that should tell you exactly how useless he is," Ronan growled.

Rian entered the cell, Crystal, Flinn and Jasper following him, Daray guarding the door. "Or how useful he is. They did not even attempt to save him. They took the other two, but left him behind."

"How does that make him useful?" Jasper asked.

"There is a chance he will want to get even with them for leaving him behind," Rian said.

"We should have kept them at my place. Then I would have had the chance to talk to them for more than half an hour," Ronan said. "But you had to interfere."

Amber shook the Pliethin and it bounced at the end of the chain. "How can they use these?"

"Can we all use them?" Jasper asked.

Amber stared at her brother. Could they? She slid her fingers into the cage.

"No." Ronan reached for her.

Amber stepped backwards, trying to avoid him. Everything went hazy. Another step away from Ronan who had stopped mid step had her feeling like she was pushing her way through water. "I'm in the Void?"

"Looks like it," Crystal said.

"She's still there?" Kade demanded.

"Yeah." Crystal pointed in Amber's direction. "Right there."

"Get out here this minute," Ronan ordered.

Amber looked at her fingers inside the cage, pressed against the Pliethin. There was a sensation of pins constantly pricking her fingers. Should she let it go? How was she meant to get out of the Void. "I'm not quite sure what to do. Do I just let the Pliethin go?"

"Amber wants to know if she should let the Pliethin go," Crystal said.

"No." Ronan, Kade and Rian all spoke at once, moving towards the place Crystal had pointed to.

"We don't know what will happen if you do," Kade said. "When people who can't walk the Void are left in it, they rarely survive."

Maybe entering the Void hadn't been the best idea. "Then what the hell am I meant to do?" Amber demanded. She walked forward, reaching for Kade. Her hand and the chain passed through him. A shiver went through her.

"Amber?" Kade held up his hand as if trying to touch her.

"Yeah, she's right in front of you," Crystal said.

"Then get over there and drag her out," Ronan said.

"Don't even think about it," Flinn said. "What if my mage gets stuck in there too?"

Crystal strode towards Amber. "Then you'll have to get another one. I'm not about to leave my best friend stuck in the Void." Crystal took hold of Amber's hand. "Let go of the Pliethin."

Amber willingly did. The world came back into focus and she threw her arms around Crystal. "Probably not the smartest thing I've ever done."

"I want one of them," Jasper said.

"We don't even know how to use them." Amber

drew away from Crystal, the cage banging against her leg. "Don't even think about it."

Kade tugged her to him. "Like you shouldn't have?"

Amber couldn't help smiling. She shrugged. "Maybe."

"Give me the Pliethin." Ronan held out his hand.

Amber held the cage behind her. "It's mine. I captured it."

"And you were the one who nearly got stuck in the Void with it," Ronan said.

"It's still mine."

"Don't use it," Ronan said.

She met his gaze, trying to think of how to reply. She didn't want to get stuck in the Void, but being able to use the Void without a Gold would be very useful. "Were mages able to travel the Void back before they were all killed off?"

"Don't try and distract me. It's not going to work, Amber. Do not use the Pliethin."

"I wasn't. I want to know. And I still do."

"Argue this later. We need to put Stanley somewhere more secure," Flinn said.

"My place," Ronan said. "This place isn't secure enough."

"We only had one cell that was protected from

trackers and Void walkers. We put the unknown man in it," Rian said.

"They shouldn't have been able to find them." Amber glanced around the room. "They had no dragon blood in them. I couldn't smell it. They shouldn't have been able to mentally call for help. Unless there's things about Knight Mages you haven't told us."

Ronan shook his head. "You know everything I know about them."

"Which doesn't mean anything," Flinn said.

"Grandad is definitely going to say no then," Jasper said.

Amber shrugged. "It doesn't matter. We've got other things to worry about right now. How safe is Temolae Keep? And what about Roy? Where is he?"

"Safe," Rian said.

Amber was relieved. She had enough problems without having to worry about what would happen if Roy was harmed while in her care. "Make sure he stays that way." She mentally searched the area. None of the enemy had returned. "All right. Take Stanley to your place. I'll be over tomorrow to have a talk to him." And he better talk. She wasn't in the mood for games.

"Hand over the Pliethin." Ronan stepped forward, holding out his hand.

Amber shook her head. "No. It's mine. Look, I'm not about to do anything with it tonight. I'm tired and I still need to see if I can heal Miles."

"And talk to Mum. We need to let her know we're okay," Jasper said.

"You can bring it with you tomorrow then," Ronan said. "I'll expect you as soon as you wake up."

"After breakfast," Amber said.

"Make sure you do." Ronan held her gaze a moment then disappeared.

Chapter Thirteen

Amber sensed Ronan step out of the Void next to Stanley and then the two of them vanished into the Void. "Jasper, you can get Daray to take you to see Mum and then he can take you home when you're ready. You can let her know I'm okay. There's no way I'm talking to her again tonight." When Jasper nodded, she turned to Rian. "Where's Miles?"

"Several doors down from your room."

She held her hand out to Kade. "Can you take me to our room?" As Kade took her into the Void, she caught a glimpse of Crystal turning to Rian with a smile, Flinn glaring at them before he disappeared too. Flinn was just going to have to learn to deal with it. He didn't own Crystal.

Kade continued to hold her hand. "Do you want me to come with you to see Miles?"

"No, I'll be right."

He stared at her for several minutes before he spoke. "Don't use the Pliethin. At least not on your own."

"I didn't think it'd work. I mean, I wasn't trying to make it work. Just trying to get away from Ronan."

"That's all it takes. Not wanting to be in that space."

"Okay." She took a step away from him, still holding his hand. Another step and she let him go, watching as he disappeared. Searching the castle she couldn't find him and wondered where he'd gone. Was he in the Void nearby or had he gone somewhere else? Mentally shrugging, she glanced around the room, trying to decide where to leave her Pliethin.

She crossed the room to the window and wrapped the chain around the rod the curtains hung from. Her gaze was drawn to the soft glow coming from the cage, the hum of energy reminding her of the first time she'd realised she had a connection with Kade. It seemed so long ago. A smile tugged at the corner of her mouth as she touched the base of the cage, spinning it gently. An eternity ago. In another lifetime. A life she no longer missed. She spun the Pliethin's cage once more before she strode from the room, mentally searching the area. Only Miles was nearby.

Opening the door, she paused, watching him as he remained seated on the edge of the bed, staring at the lit lamp on the set of drawers beside the bed. His green eyes were nearly unblinking, his shoulders were slumped and his brown hair was neatly trimmed. Another search of the area showed they were still alone. Unless of course there was someone in the Void watching her. But she couldn't worry about that. She had to focus on trying to heal Miles.

Crossing the room, she stood beside him. He didn't move. His gaze remained on the lamp. Hesitantly she reached out and rested her hand on his head. How was she meant to go about fixing him? Finding the dragon blood in him, she followed it through his system, trying to find any problems. But she didn't know enough about the human body, especially the brain, to know what might be wrong.

Giving up on that, she tried to heal him in general. Energy drained from her and she staggered, falling backwards as he leapt to his feet. She winced as she collided with the floor, struggling to rise. Before she could, Miles launched himself at her, lightning pooling in his hands. She rolled out of the way, sensing Daray come out of the Void. "Don't hurt him."

Miles threw lightning at Daray. One hit him, but he kept coming, tackling Miles to the ground. Footsteps could be heard in the hallway and Amber jumped to her feet, mentally checking who it was. Rian burst into the room, Cooper and Elliot on his heels.

"Let him go." Elliot ran towards Miles and Daray.

"He attacked us," Amber said.

"What did you do to him?" Elliot demanded.

Miles stilled. "Elliot?"

"Let him go." Elliot helped Miles up. "Are you okay?"

"Where are we? What's going on?" Miles looked around the room. "Cooper?"

"We're safe," Cooper said.

"They're dragons." Miles gestured towards Rian and Daray.

Cooper nodded. "Yeah, but we're safe."

Kade stepped out of the Void, reaching for Amber. "Are you okay?"

She nodded, drawing energy from one of her bracelets, still feeling drained after healing Miles. At least she hoped he was healed. "Yeah."

"What happened?" Kade asked.

"I'm not sure." She eyed Miles. "Why did you attack me?"

"You did something to me. I don't know what, but my head exploded with pain," Miles said.

"You said you wouldn't hurt us," Elliot said.

"I didn't. I was trying to heal him. And look." She gestured towards Miles. "He isn't staring off into space like he's not in his own body."

"I wasn't," Miles said.

"What do you mean?" Amber asked.

"When the dragons learned I could split my consciousness they had me checking out the defences of their enemies," Miles said.

She still didn't know what he was talking about. "What exactly does that mean?"

"I travel with my mind while still having a slight awareness of my body and what's happening to it. Although the longer I'm split the harder it is to focus on what is happening around my body until it's like being caught in the dark. Everything was dark. I tried to find a way out of that warehouse, but I got lost. I had no way to get back," Miles said.

"You tried to kill yourself," Cooper said.

Miles nodded. "I was lost. I had no way to get back. I didn't want to be stuck like that forever." He looked around the room again. "How did I get here?"

Ronan came out of the Void, his arms crossed as he leaned against the wall near the door. "Interesting. This could be useful."

"Didn't you hear him?" Elliot demanded. "He couldn't get back. I'm not going to let you do that to him."

Ronan pushed away from the wall. "And you think you can stop me?"

Amber stepped between Ronan and Elliot, facing Ronan. "Miles won't be doing anything that endangers him. If he learns how to use his ability and wants to help us, he can."

Ronan grabbed Amber's shoulder and took her through the Void before she could pull away from him. They came out in his family crypt. "Stop arguing with me all the time."

"Maybe I should say the same." A message came through on her phone and she checked it, sending a quick reply to let Kade know she was okay. "And stop bringing me here. The last place I want to be," she checked the time, "at one a.m. is hanging out with the dead."

"Then stop doing stupid things or you'll permanently be with them."

"It wasn't stupid. I was healing Miles."

"Then why'd he attack you? Rian rang Kade to

tell him Miles was attacking you and to get back immediately. How did that happen if all you were doing was healing him?"

She shrugged. "He was confused." She paused. "Why was Kade with you?"

"That's unimportant. Are you trying to get yourself killed? That would really piss me off."

Amber sighed. "No. Look, I was just trying to heal him. You heard what he said. He's been out of his head for ages. Literally. And I'm okay. He missed me. None of them can fight."

"And what if he'd been able to fight? What then?"

"Can we drop this already? I had it all under control. He wouldn't have hit me. I'm not an idiot. As if I'd stay still for him. Now why was Kade with you?"

Ronan pointed a finger at her. "Our deal only counts if you get yourself killed fighting Hell Hounds."

She started to argue, but stopped herself. It'd be a waste of breath. Ronan wasn't about to give any more than he'd already agreed to. "I don't plan on getting myself killed. In this war or at any other time. Now take me home. I'm tired and want to get some sleep before sunrise."

Ronan eyed her. "You've changed, kitten."

"No, not really. It just took me a bit to get used to everything." Then she shrugged. "Well, maybe I'm not always saying things the moment I think them." She grinned. "I hear that can get you killed."

Ronan chuckled. "Are you certain you're not interested in Rian?"

"Positive." She started to say he was Crystal's then stopped.

"What?"

"Nothing. Another one of those comments it's not necessary to speak." If he didn't know, she wasn't about to tell him about Rian and Crystal.

Ronan remained quiet for a moment. "Have you found enough humans yet?"

"How many is enough?"

"Fifty, a hundred, a hundred and fifty." He shrugged. "It's war. Some are sure to die and need to be replaced."

"I've got nearly fifty."

"That's a start." He held out his hand. "I'll take you home."

Amber held his gaze a moment longer. She was slowly becoming accustomed to seeing gold eyes instead of pale blue. "We can make more mages again later? Ones that I can choose."

Ronan nodded.

Feeling more relieved about her mother not jumping at the chance to become a mage, Amber took his hand. "Good."

Ronan took her through the Void to her room. *"Be careful."* He disappeared.

Behind her she could feel the energy of the Pliethin. She was trying to be careful, but sometimes war wasn't the place for being cautious. Mentally searching for Kade, she found him near Rian, wishing she could travel through the Void to them since they were on the other side of the castle from her. Turning, she looked at the Pliethin. It was tempting, but probably not the best idea.

Instead of trying to use the Pliethin, she spoke to Kade. *"I'm home, in our room."*

Kade appeared in front of her, blocking her view of the Pliethin. "Are you okay?"

"Yeah. Why were you with Ronan?"

"I was checking on Stanley, making sure he didn't kill him."

"I'm half tempted to say 'let him'. We're probably not going to get anything useful out of him. And I have no idea what to do with him once we're finished questioning him."

"Rian seems to think we'll learn something."

She shrugged, looking past him to the Pliethin.

"Will it be okay in there? I mean, I don't know, does it need to eat or something?"

"No. It gains energy from its environment." Kade looked towards the Pliethin, reaching out a hand to brush his fingers against the wooden bars. "It's not living like us."

Amber removed the chain from the curtain rod, holding the Pliethin up to peer in at it. She sniffed at the cage. "I can smell dragon-leather." She ran her fingers over the timber. "I can't feel it though."

Kade stepped close, his hand cupping hers so he could bring the cage up to his face. He frowned. "I wonder if that helps it work."

"And blood. I can smell dragon blood too." She tilted the cage. "I think it's on the ceiling and floor of the cage."

"We might be able to make some of these ourselves," Kade said. "That's if we can figure out how to use them safely. Promise me you won't use it alone."

"Only if you promise to help me learn how to use it."

Kade nodded. "Sounds fair."

"Now?"

He chuckled. "How about we wait until after we've had a sleep."

Even though she was tired, she really wanted to figure out how to use the Pliethin. She wanted to be able to travel the Void without any help.

"Come on, Amber. At least a few hours sleep."

Holding the Pliethin by the chain with one hand, she brushed at the shadows under his left eye, curving her hand down across his cheek and finally resting against his neck. "I suppose. But I don't want to leave it too long. Things are probably going to get crazy again soon."

"You'll get used to it. Things are regularly crazy." He took the Pliethin from her and hung it from the curtain rod, turning back to her with a grin. "We're dragons. We live for crazy."

Chapter Fourteen

Amber groaned as she tried to find her phone, her eyes still closed.

"Answer it," Kade growled from beside her.

"Trying," she muttered, her hand finally landing on the phone instead of the surface of the chest of drawers at the side of the bed. Squinting at the phone screen she saw it was her mother. "What?"

"I'll do it."

Amber pushed at the sheets as she struggled to sit up. "What?"

"I'll become a Dragon Mage. And Gary. He's to become one too."

"You will?" Maybe she was still asleep. No, that couldn't be possible. When she dreamt, it was always of blood. So she had to be awake. There wasn't a single drop of blood in sight.

"But I won't be joining the dragons. Or Knights.

I'm only doing this to learn how to protect myself from any dragons or Knights that might come after me to get at you."

"Okay."

"And I need someone to teach me how to fight."

"Rian."

"Isn't he your bodyguard?"

"No, my first warrior. But don't worry, he won't leave me unprotected." She paused. "Thank you."

"And I don't think you should turn your father into one either. Look what a mess he made of things by chasing after Vikki."

Now probably wasn't a good time to explain that Vikki had deliberately broken them up. Never would probably be the perfect time to tell her mother. "Uhm, okay." She could worry about her father later, but it was probably safer for him if he was kept as far away from dragons as possible. She also didn't want to risk her mother changing her mind. Besides, he knew nothing about this world and she really didn't have time to wait for him to get over his shock. There were far too many other things to focus on right now.

"When?"

Amber struggled to keep up with the conversation. "What?"

"When do you want to do this?"

"Tomorrow. Ronan's making the new Dragon Mages tomorrow."

"I guess you'll send someone for us."

"Yeah." Why had she stayed up so late? Maybe a bit more sleep might have helped her keep up with the conversation. "Have you told Jay?"

"No. I'll ring him now. See you tomorrow, Amber."

"Okay." She stared at her phone after her mother had hung up.

"You don't look happy about this," Kade said.

She met his gaze. "Yeah, I am. I'm just…" her voice trailed off as she tried to think how to explain her feelings. "Surprised. No, confused. I thought for sure she'd take a lot more convincing." She dropped back against her pillow. "I guess that means we've only got one more mage to find."

"It'll have to wait. Ronan expects us there after breakfast, remember?"

"I'm not hungry yet."

Kade chuckled. "Dragon." The word was an endearment.

Amber rolled onto her side, smiling as she faced him. Before she could speak, a message came through on her phone. She laughed as she read her brother's message. *Am I a genius or what?* She tilted the phone so Kade could read it. When Kade chuckled, she smiled, rising from the bed. "I want to learn how to use the Pliethin before we visit Ronan."

"Right now?"

Amber nodded, reaching for her weapons that were on the floor beside the bed. "Yep." Once her weapons were in place and she'd slid her phone into a pocket, she crossed the room to take the Pliethin down. Holding onto the chain she faced Kade, who had his sword at his side and was pulling on a dragon-leather vest to match his trousers. "How do we do this?"

Kade strode towards her, wrapping his arm around her waist, still facing her. "You don't let go of the Pliethin and I don't let go of you. That way neither of us should get lost in the Void."

"Okay. Then what do I do?"

"Exactly what you did yesterday."

"It'd be nice if you could be helpful," she muttered as she pushed her fingers into the cage. She had no idea what she'd done yesterday. Other than not wanting Ronan to get the Pliethin from her. She took a step backwards, Kade moving with her. Nothing happened.

"Try and feel like you're stepping through a doorway."

"How do you feel that? It's more of a visual thing."

"No, it's not. There's a sensation to it. Going from one place to another."

"Great." She glared at the Pliethin, trying to figure out how to feel a sensation that didn't really exist. She took another step backwards. Again nothing. Swearing she took a step forward, pressing against Kade. That didn't help either. She closed her eyes. A doorway. She could do this. Somehow. Picturing a doorway, she stepped backwards. Opening her eyes she didn't see any difference. "That's a stupid explanation. It didn't work."

"Maybe it's different when you're a mage. You did it yesterday. You should be able to do it again today."

"Maybe you're the problem."

"Don't even think about going into the Void by yourself again."

"What about when you first went into the Void. Did you do it by yourself?"

"That's different."

"How is it?"

"I knew what I was doing."

"Then tell me so I'll know what to do."

"I've already told you. Focus on the sensation of stepping through a doorway. Then step through it. If you move when you're first learning, it's easier. You can move backwards or forwards, it doesn't matter. Then you do the same to come out into the place you came in from."

"Fine. You and me walking through a doorway." She took a step backwards and felt like the air around her thickened. "I did it." She grinned. "I did it." Her grin faded. "It was me, wasn't it? You didn't help."

"I didn't help." Kade grinned. "Even though you were driving me crazy with your attempts. Now how about you leave the Void."

"Okay. Stepping out of the Void." She took another step backwards, but nothing happened. Maybe it had been a fluke. No, she wouldn't accept that. She thought about how she'd entered the Void, then smiled. "You and me." She took a step backwards, coming out of the Void. "It is your fault."

"What's my fault?"

"I can't just think of walking through a doorway, or the sensation or whatever you want to call it. I have to think of the two of us. You actually were stopping me from entering." She frowned. "I wonder…" her voice trailed off. Surely it couldn't be that easy.

"What are you thinking?"

"Okay, if I think of staying here, not moving, you try and take us into the Void."

"Now?"

Amber nodded, trying to think of ways to anchor herself to the spot. She swore when they entered the Void. "Take us back out again." When they were out, she said, "Okay, count to five then try to enter the Void." This time instead of an anchor, she focused on being rooted to the spot. The scents of the area, the sounds and the sensation of being in this particular room. Time passed and she started to ask when he was about to try. They entered the Void. "Oh, it didn't work."

"Yeah, it did. I was trying to shift us for nearly a minute before I managed to."

"It worked?"

Kade nodded.

She let go of the Pliethin and threw her arms around him, his still around her waist. "I did it?"

"Yeah and you better not let go of the Pliethin if it's you who enters the Void."

"I'm not an idiot." She couldn't stop grinning. "Take us out of the Void so I can try again. This time I want to see if I can do it without the Pliethin."

She couldn't. No matter how hard she tried, Kade was able to take her into the Void. The moment she touched the Pliethin, he couldn't. Then she practised entering and leaving the Void a few more times.

"I wonder if you could stop someone taking you into the Void."

Kade nodded. "Only if I'm stronger then them. Mental strength, not physical strength."

"Does that mean I'm mentally stronger than you?"

Kade chuckled. "You wish. No, it'll be because of the Pliethin. It's energy. That's far stronger than most minds."

"I wonder if it'd be stronger than Ronan's mind."

"I don't know."

"Then let's go and have breakfast so we can find out." With Kade's arm still around her, she touched her fingers to the Pliethin and took them into the Void. "Now how do I get us to the dining room?"

"You can't. You haven't entered the Void from there before. You'll only be able to take us to the dungeon."

"How do I do that?"

"It's a thread. Like a sliver of light. Can you see it?"

"Maybe."

"Then take hold of it."

"Both my hands are full."

"Not with your hands. Your mind."

"I really wish you'd learn to explain yourself a lot better."

"Maybe you're just not good at understanding dragon things."

"I doubt it." She looked around, seeing what looked like a pinpoint of light. Staring at it, she tried to see it better. The pinpoint became a thread. "Okay, now what?"

"Draw it to yourself. Picture the place you want to go and tug it to you with the thread."

She tugged it towards herself and the dungeon seemed to come towards her in a rush. Swaying, she was glad that the heaviness of the air kept her on her feet. As soon as she was steady, she stepped out of the Void. Grinning, she let go of the Pliethin to throw her arms around Kade and kiss him. "I did it."

"Yep." His arms tightened around her and he took them through the Void to the dining room. "Now let's have breakfast before I starve to death."

She laughed. "It's going to take more than an hour to starve."

"Try a couple of hours."

"It wasn't." She drew away slightly so she could check the time. "It was. I didn't realise." Her stomach grumbled as the smell of breakfast reminded her that she needed to eat. "Okay. Breakfast and then we'll see Ronan. I want to see if I can keep him from taking me through the Void." She grinned. "I really hope I can."

"That would have been handy against Tahmid."

Sitting at the table, Amber nodded. "We need to figure out how to make these cages. Jasper needs one."

"I would have thought you'd want to see if they worked for your first warrior."

She started to say that wouldn't be a problem shortly, then stopped. It wasn't time to let Kade or Crystal know what Rian planned to do. "I'll tell him about it."

As soon as they'd finished breakfast, Amber let Rian know they were going to see Ronan. Kade took them through the Void to Ronan's rooftop garden, coming out beside the water garden. They were alone.

"Hold onto me so I can take us back into the Void to get a string for here."

"A pathway."

"String, pathway, it doesn't matter what they're called." She slid her fingers into the cage, stepping backwards with Kade's arm around her. Grinning at how much easier it was getting, she took another step backwards and left the Void.

Ronan appeared beside them. "What are you doing?" His gaze was drawn to Amber's fingers still pushed between the bars of the cage. "And why are you using the Pliethin?"

Amber withdrew her fingers from the cage, stepping away from Kade. "I wasn't doing it alone. Kade was helping me."

"You're as bad as each other."

"No we're not. Actually, I was hoping you could help me test something."

"Not if it's to do with that." Ronan gestured towards the cage.

"I want to see if I can stop you from taking me into the Void. Kade can't shift me."

"He's a child. Of course he can't shift you."

Amber smiled. "What about you?"

Ronan closed the distance between them. "As if I'd have a problem shifting you." His hand shot out and he grabbed hold of her arm.

Before Amber had a chance to touch the Pliethin again, Ronan took her through the Void to his crypt. "I wasn't ready."

"Do you think your enemies will wait for you to be ready?"

"Of course not, but I'm still learning. Give me until the count of ten before you try to shift me. Please?"

Ronan held her gaze for a moment before he nodded.

As much as she didn't like to stay in the crypt, Amber focused on rooting herself to the spot. The air felt like it tried to close in on her as she fought to hold onto the location. Then she was torn out of it, standing in the Void looking through a haze at the crypt. They came out of the Void and back into the crypt almost instantly. "It didn't work."

"In a way it did."

"What way?"

"I couldn't shift you straight through the Void to the location I wanted to take you to. I had to bring you into the Void. And it was a struggle to do that with the way the Void kept trying to force us out of it. Most dragons wouldn't be planning to shift into the Void, they'd aim to shift you to another location through the Void. It'll give you time to call for help."

"Does that mean I get to keep my Pliethin?"

"For now." Ronan took them through the Void, bringing them out at his water garden.

Kade looked from one to the other. "It didn't work?"

Amber repeated what Ronan had told her. "It felt odd. Like the air was trying to suffocate me or something. I mean, I could still breathe, it just felt like it was trying to press in on me."

"Enough of this. Stanley is being highly

uncooperative. I thought you might like to help get information out of him," Ronan said.

"What makes you think I'll be able to get him to talk?" Amber asked.

"I don't." Ronan grinned. "I want you there so I don't have to be as careful about keeping him alive. That will be your job."

Amber shook her head. "Oh no you don't. I'm not going to stand there and watch you torture him."

"Do you really think he's going to tell you everything just because you ask?"

"Probably not everything. But have you tried asking?"

Ronan looked towards Kade. "Have you taught her nothing?"

"Don't go looking at him. You're the one I should be asking that question of. Most of what I've learned, I've learned from you."

"Then you're not a very good student," Ronan said.

Amber laughed softly. "A lot of my teachers have said that over the years."

Ronan pointed a finger at her. "This is not a game. We need all the information we can gather before we attack."

"Why don't Amber and I see what we can do?" Kade asked.

Ronan held his gaze for a moment, before he nodded. "I'm sure you can find the way. Or if you can't Daray knows where the room is." Ronan disappeared into the Void.

Chapter Fifteen

Amber glared at the spot where Ronan had been. That was such an annoying habit. She held back a sigh, glancing around. She wondered if Ronan was right and Daray was in the Void watching her. Probably. She headed inside, Kade at her side. Knowing Rian, Daray would be following her.

When they reached the room, Amber tried the door and found it unlocked. She doubted Ronan would have left it unlocked and guessed he'd been there before them. She searched the area for Ronan and not finding him nearby, searched further afield. He wasn't in her world. She guessed he'd returned to the dragon world. Swinging the door fully open, she remained in the doorway staring at Stanley who stood near a stool, a heavy chain on his ankle. The room was again empty of furnishings.

"Have you come to gloat?" Stanley snarled.

Amber wasn't sure how to answer that. Stanley looked a mess. Bruises, broken skin and dried blood. For once she wasn't tempted to heal someone. "They didn't even try to rescue you. Your so called friends just left you in our dungeon."

Stanley glared at her, remaining silent.

"They went straight for Wayne and the other man, but didn't even bother with you."

"Why protect people who wouldn't bother protecting you?" Kade asked.

Again Stanley remained silent.

Amber stared at him. Obviously asking wasn't going to get her any information. But it looked like Ronan's methods hadn't worked either. "You know, Ronan wanted me here so I could heal you. So that no matter what he did while trying to make you talk, you wouldn't be able to die."

"You're wasting your time. I'll never help dragons."

Amber nodded "I didn't think so. I don't know whether to tell Ronan to kill you and stop wasting time on you, or let you starve. Like you would have done to me." She stared at Stanley a moment, pretty certain she wouldn't be able to bring herself to suggest either option. "Do you even know what's going on?"

"If you knew anything, they wouldn't have left you behind," Kade said.

"Did you know them?" Amber decided to play a hunch. "I mean obviously you knew Wayne and Martin, but did you know the other man? Or did you just blindly follow him?"

"Do you know every single person you work with? Martin and Wayne knew him. That was enough for me."

She wished she'd been wrong. "And what about the Hell Hounds? Did they tell you about them?" Amber then spoke directly to Kade. *"Can you go and get some of the pictures?"*

"I'm not about to leave you alone with him. Ask Daray."

"You made them up. Martin would have told me about them, if they existed."

"Daray." Amber was relieved when Daray came out of the Void behind her. She looked over her shoulder to where he stood in the corridor. *"Bring me some pictures of the Hell Hounds."*

Daray nodded, disappearing back into the Void.

Amber faced Stanley, moving closer to him. "Or maybe you just aren't important enough for them to tell you about the Hell Hounds."

"Nice try. I'm not about to fall for that," Stanley sneered.

Daray stepped out of the Void, entered the room and handed two pieces of paper to Amber. He remained at her shoulder.

Amber held the two pictures up in front of Stanley. "This is what's coming."

Stanley laughed. "Sure. I'll look forward to meeting them."

She hadn't expected him to believe, but she'd thought it was worth trying. "Vikki was the first one to tell me about them." She handed the pictures back to Daray.

"Don't you even speak her name. You murdered her."

She started to argue against his comment, then stopped. She hadn't needed to kill Vikki. Again she felt the anger and pain she'd experience when Vikki had told her Kade was dead. She nodded. "Yeah. Maybe. But that doesn't change the fact that the Hell Hounds are coming."

"We're wasting our time, Amber," Kade said.

Amber continued to stare at Stanley. Everyone was right. Stanley probably knew nothing. They wouldn't have left him behind if he was important. But they had learned something. "The Hounds are coming, Stanley. And you're going to wish you had listened to us." Amber turned to Kade, holding out her hand. *"Take me to Ronan's water garden."* She made sure both Kade and Daray heard her.

Kade took her through the Void, bringing her out beside the water feature. "Why here?"

Amber took out her phone, dialling Ronan's number. "Because we need to talk about Martin."

Ronan stepped out of the Void, his phone still ringing. "Very nice, kitten."

"What was?" She disconnected the call, returning her phone to her pocket.

"Martin."

She should have known that Ronan was in the Void and not in the dragons' world. "I thought so too. So what are we going to do about it?"

Ronan grinned. "I think we need to have a talk to Martin."

"If he's a Knight Mage, kidnapping him will have them attacking us again," Kade said.

"No, we don't want to kidnap him. And we need others there. Other Knights. Stanley doesn't know about the Hell Hounds. My grandparents didn't know about the Hell Hounds. Not until we told them. So why don't they? Why do only a handful of Knights know?"

"What are you thinking of doing?" Ronan asked.

Amber slowly shook her head. "I'm not sure. But I think we need to meet with him. Talk to him face-to-face. And I think there are others who need to hear what he has to say."

"What others?" Kade asked.

"My grandparents. Isaac. I don't know." She shrugged. "Maybe there are others, but I wouldn't know who." Isaac probably did. "I'll see my grandparents first. Then Isaac."

"You better not screw this up. I'm relying on you to do this right, kitten."

She nodded. *"I haven't failed yet."* She couldn't afford to.

"Don't go getting cocky or you will fail."

She grinned. *"Remember, I've got too many relying on me for failure to ever be an option."*

Ronan handed her a business card sized piece of cardboard, which he drew from a pocket. It had a handwritten address. "Have your humans here by eight o'clock tomorrow night."

Amber stared at the card. "What's here?"

"The building I held Cooper in. Do not be late."

Amber was tempted to point out that he wasn't always on time. Instead, she nodded. That wasn't going to give her much time to notify everyone as well as see her grandparents and Isaac. Maybe she shouldn't have spent the morning playing with the Pliethin. She'd have to ask Rian and Crystal to organise everybody while she spoke to her grandparents. "I'll see you then." She held out a hand to Kade, hoping Daray, who she guessed was in the Void, figured out where they'd go. *"Can you take me to Temolae Keep?"*

"Are you sure you don't want to try?" Kade took her hand as Ronan vanished.

Amber laughed. She hadn't thought about that. *"Sure, why not?"* She pushed her fingers inside the cage, feeling the sting of the Pliethin as she came in contact with it. Taking a step away from Kade she entered the Void, drawing the thread to her that would take them to Temolae Keep. When she stepped out of the Void and into their bedroom, she let go of the Pliethin to throw her arms around Kade. "I did it."

"I didn't doubt you could."

"I have to talk to Rian and Crystal, ring Isaac to organise a meeting and then we can go and see my grandparents."

"I'm sure they're going to be thrilled to see us."

"Aren't they always?"

It didn't take Amber long to find Rian and Crystal.

She met with them in the planning room, leaving Daray who left the Void when they entered the room, to guard the door and make sure they weren't disturbed. They agreed to notify everyone. There would only be a couple that they'd have to visit, which Rian would do with the help of a Gold while Crystal rang or emailed everyone on their list. Amber also told them about Martin and what they suspected.

Once Rian and Crystal left the planning room, Amber rang Charles. When he took so long to answer, she began to think he was ignoring her.

"You had better not be calling to try and convince me to become a Knight Mage. I'm not weak like Donna."

Her first instinct was to defend her mother. She resisted the urge. Barely. "No. I've come across other information I thought you should have."

"Has this information come from dragons?"

"It came from a Knight."

"What is it?"

"I want to see you in person, you and Grandma, if you want the information."

There was nearly a minute's silence before Charles replied. "I'll be home in twenty minutes. Meet me there."

"Both of you?"

"Yes." Charles hung up.

Amber leaned forward to rest her head on the table. "Why does everything have to be so complicated?"

Kade chuckled. "Things aren't even close to being complicated yet."

"Bloody Dragons," Amber muttered as she rose to her feet. "And Knights. You're all as bad as each other."

Kade laughed, reaching out and drawing her close. "You wouldn't have us any other way."

She started to protest, then smiled. "Maybe." She drew away from him. "I need to ring Isaac."

It was a much easier call than the one to her grandparent's had been. He suggested meeting her at his sister's house once she'd finished seeing her grandparents. After hanging up, she stared at her phone for a moment, wondering if she was doing the right thing. But what other options were there? She rose to her feet, holding her hand out to Kade. "Ready?"

When they arrived out the front of her grandparents' house, Amber wondered if she should have brought her brother. Jasper was much better at getting their grandmother to see his point of view than she was. She was only good at getting her grandmother to argue.

Charles opened the door when Amber knocked. He stood silently in the doorway for nearly a minute, before he stepped to the side and let them enter, closing the door behind them. He led the way to a lounge room where Helen sat waiting for them in a single seater armchair. Charles sat in the only other single seater armchair, leaving the double one for Amber and Kade.

Amber wasn't certain how to start. She looked from Helen to Charles, then back to Helen. They probably weren't going to believe her, but she had to try anyway.

"Well?" Charles demanded.

Amber glanced at him before she turned her attention back to her grandmother. "I learned that Martin knows about Knight Mages."

"Who told you?" Charles asked.

"Well, they didn't exactly come out and say that he knows, but he was working with one. We think he knows about them and is involved with their organisation," Amber said.

"So you're making this accusation because of who he associates with," Charles said.

Amber shrugged. It sounded bad when it was put like that. "We haven't accused him of anything. Well, not really. We need people, Knights, willing to hide nearby and listen when we ask him about it. He may not say anything, but just in case he does, we want someone there who'll know what to do about it," Amber said.

"Who else will be there?" Helen asked.

"The only person we've asked at the moment is you," Kade said.

Amber almost glanced towards Kade. "Do you really trust Martin? Just because he's the High Protector, doesn't mean he's trustworthy."

"He's more trustworthy than your dragons," Charles said.

"My dragons helped ransom you," Amber said.

"What would you know about it? It's policy. Being High Protector, doesn't change anything," Charles snapped.

Amber looked from Charles, then to Helen again, her gaze returning to Charles. "Why do I feel like I'm missing something here?"

Helen shook her head when Charles looked towards her. "I didn't say a word."

"Well?" Amber asked.

"Nothing that concerns you," Charles said.

"Are you sure it doesn't affect what we were asking of you?" Kade asked.

"I will come with you," Charles said. "But if nothing happens, Martin isn't to know I was there."

"I'll come too," Helen said.

"I'll organise for you to watch from the Void," Amber said.

"When?" Charles asked.

"I don't know." Amber shrugged. "I'll let you know when he agrees to meet with me."

Charles rose to his feet. "No matter what we learn, it won't change anything between us. Like I told Donna, if she chooses the dragons then we have no other family."

Amber jumped to her feet. "Being a mage doesn't mean Mum has sided with the dragons. How can you be so... so-" Amber threw her hands up with a growl. "She loves you." Amber jabbed a finger in his direction. "You can't do that to her." She thought of how excited her mother had been about seeing her father for the first time since she was a toddler.

"Don't tell me what I can or can't do. I'll never forgive the dragons for what they stole from me. Roger, Donna, even you and your brother, should have been Knights. Instead, they've stolen you too."

"No, they haven't. You're throwing us away." Amber started to stride from the room. She paused at the doorway. "I'll let you know when I'm meeting

Martin." She held his gaze a moment. There were other words she wanted to speak. Angry words. But it was pointless. He wouldn't listen. He'd already made up his mind. With a glance towards her grandmother, she left the room, striding towards the front door, Kade at her side.

She still had to speak with Isaac. Maybe she shouldn't have organised to meet with him straight after her grandparents. She wasn't in the mood to see anyone else. When they stepped outside, Kade took her hand, taking her through the Void. She was relieved to find herself in their bedroom at Temolae Keep. "Why here?"

"I thought you might want a minute before we visit Isaac."

Amber smiled, sliding her arms around his waist, resting her head on his shoulder. "Yeah, I do." Behind him she could feel the Pliethin pulsing with energy and was tempted to take it with her. But she shouldn't need it. Not tonight. Breathing out heavily, she relaxed against Kade.

"Let me know when you're ready to go."

"I will."

"We probably don't want to leave it too late."

She chuckled, drawing back enough to be able to

meet his gaze. "Is this your way of telling me to hurry up?"

Kade grinned. "No, just pointing out the facts."

"Okay. Let's go."

"Eliza's kitchen?"

She hesitated, then nodded. Drawing away from him as soon as they arrived, she grinned in greeting at the glare Amos sent towards her as he stopped pacing the room.

Chapter Sixteen

"What's wrong with the front door." Eliza rose from the table, where she sat across from Isaac, also glaring at Amber.

She ignored the question and faced Isaac. "I'm going to try and set up a meeting with Martin. I'd like you there in the Void to hear what he has to say."

"You're not leaving me behind," Amos said at the same time as Eliza said, "I'm coming too."

"My grandparents will be in the Void also."

Isaac nodded. "When are you going to organise this?"

"As soon as possible."

"What makes you think you can get Martin to admit to anything?" Amos demanded.

"I may not be able to, but I'm going to try," Amber said.

"What if he's guilty of using the Knights for his

own agenda?" Isaac asked. "What do you plan to do then?"

Amber held his gaze for a moment, thinking over her answer before she spoke. "I don't plan to do anything. I'm not a Knight. That'll be something you lot will have to figure out."

"We're not idiots," Amos muttered. "What are you really up to?"

Smiling, she faced Amos. "Why do you always think I've got some secret plan? It's you Knights that seem to be planning trouble at the moment. Or at least Martin is."

"Dragons aren't innocent either," Amos said. He glanced towards his brother and shook his head before turning away and began pacing again.

Amber wished she could ask what Isaac had said, but she knew better than to waste her breath. She turned to Isaac. "Are there any other Knights you think should be there?"

"No, the quieter we can keep this, the better."

"Okay." Amber paused. "Can I get Martin's phone number from you?"

He nodded. "I'll text it to you. His public one. Anyone can get hold of it."

"Thanks. I'll let you know when I'm meeting him."

"You're going?" Eliza asked. "You haven't even told me how Roy is."

"You ring him every day. Don't you know?"

Eliza pointed a finger in her direction. "I want to hear it from you. How is my boy?"

"My first warrior is teaching him how to fight."

"As a dragon?" Eliza demanded.

Amber shook her head. "No, but he should learn that. We're all going to need every fighting skill we've got."

"We're Knights. Stop trying to turn us into dragons," Amos growled.

Again Amber bit back the comment she wanted to make. He could deny it all he liked, but he was also part dragon. She faced Isaac. "Do you have anyone willing to be a Knight Mage?"

Isaac nodded. "My wife."

Amber shared a look with Kade. She hadn't even known Isaac was married. From the look Kade sent her, she guessed he was equally surprised.

"No." Amos and Eliza spoke at the same time.

"Are you saying she can't be trusted? She knows everything about us. If we can trust her with our secrets we can trust her with this," Isaac said.

"That wasn't what I meant," Amos said. "What if

someone finds out? They'd think she's sided with the dragons. It'd look bad for you."

"No one will find out. We'll make sure of it. But if she's right," Isaac gestured towards Amber, "Then we're going to need people who can see Hell Hounds. Before that happens we need to know what Knight Mages are capable of. We need to know if they can figure out our secret as easily as a Dragon Mage can. Lydia will be able to tell us that."

"I'll text you the address of where she needs to be tomorrow night at eight," Amber said.

Isaac nodded.

"She's not going there alone," Amos said.

"You won't be able to be in there with her, but you can wait outside," Amber said.

"How do we know she'll be safe?" Eliza's gaze travelled from Amber to Isaac. "You're a fool."

Isaac chuckled. "No. Not at all."

"What did you tell her?" Amber asked Isaac, not really expecting him to answer.

He continued to smile, shaking his head. "I'll send you Martin's number. Amos will bring Lydia to you tomorrow."

Amber held his gaze a moment longer, before she stepped closer to Kade, taking his hand when he held it out. The text came not long after they arrived in their bedroom and she sent one back to Isaac with the address Ronan had given her. She continued to stare at Martin's number. Ringing him was the last thing she wanted to do.

"Are you okay?" Kade asked.

"Yeah." She looked up from her phone. "Maybe." How was she meant to convince him to meet her?

"You don't have to ring him tonight. He mightn't be awake at this hour." He reached for her, holding her close.

"I know. But I'm afraid if I put it off I'll keep finding excuses not to ring him. Like I did with my mum."

His hand ran lightly up and down her back. "You won't. He's not important to you, so you'll make the call."

A smile tugged at the corner of her lips. He was probably right. She drew away from him. "Okay. I'm going to ring him now." Before she dialled his number, she sat on the edge of the bed.

It took Martin several rings to answer. "Hello?"

"Martin."

"What do you want?" The friendliness disappeared from his voice.

"Are you wondering where Stanley is?"

"I already know."

She paused, trying to figure out what to say next. "And that doesn't bother you?"

"I didn't say that."

A thought occurred to her and she smiled. "I'll ring you back in a minute. Someone just sent me a message I need to deal with." She hung up before he could speak.

"What are you planning? You're smiling exactly like Ronan."

Amber laughed, rising to her feet. "Good. This is a plan that should make even him proud. Take me to his house." She started to dial Ronan's number as she held out her hand.

Ronan answered immediately. "What?"

Kade took them through the Void and brought them out at Ronan's water garden. A quick search of the area showed he wasn't home. "I need to see Stanley and I need him gagged and unable to make any other noise. So he should be tied up too."

Ronan stepped out of the Void, disconnecting the call. "What are you planning, kitten?"

Amber grinned. "All sorts of things. But we need to be quick, I have to ring Martin back."

"I've sent some warriors to deal with him. Now what are you planning?"

She told Ronan of the conversation with Martin. "I want Stanley to hear it, just in case."

"You'll have to stand in the hallway. Phones don't work well in the room."

She nodded. "That's okay."

"And be careful what you admit to on the phone. Martin might record the conversation." Ronan held out his hand to her. "They've got Stanley ready."

With a glance towards Kade, who nodded, Amber took Ronan's hand. Kade came out of the Void next to them, in front of the open door. She stared in at Stanley, bound and gagged, the look in his eyes promising retribution. Satisfied he wouldn't be able to make any noise, she rang Martin again, putting the phone on speaker setting.

"Any more interruptions and you can forget about ringing back."

"No more interruptions. Anyway, we were talking about the fact that you're missing Stanley."

"I'm not missing him. Missing implies you don't know where someone is."

"And you're not bothered about where he is?"

"I'm sure he's fine where he is."

"Really? I doubt you actually think that. Particularly when I know for a fact that he's in a really unhealthy situation. Which you would also think if, as you say, you know where he is."

"Get to the point, Amber."

"Why didn't they bother taking Stanley with them? Why'd they leave him behind?"

"I have more important things to do with my time than discuss this with you."

"More important things to do than worry about one of your people?"

"If he was stupid enough to get himself into a difficult situation, that isn't my problem."

Amber kept her gaze on Stanley, watching as his expression went from retribution, to disbelief and was quickly followed by anger. "Then why did you concern yourself with the other two who got themselves into a similar situation?"

"I'm not going to say it again. Get to the point."

"I'd like to talk to you about this in person."

"Why?" Martin demanded.

"What do you mean why?"

"Exactly what I said. Why are we even discussing this now? I'm not interested in this topic."

"You can choose the location. Somewhere busy if you want, but where we can talk without anyone overhearing us."

"This matter is over. I have no further interest in it."

Worried he was about to hang up, Amber quickly spoke. "Knight Mages."

There was a moment of silence on the phone. "When did you want to meet?"

Amber watched as disbelief hit Stanley again. His shoulders slumped. She tried not to feel pity for him, but it was hard. "Tomorrow morning."

"I'll send you an address in the morning."

"Give me at least an hour's notice. Some places are difficult for me to get to."

Martin laughed. "Oh this place will certainly be difficult for you to get to."

"It better be out in the open and not somewhere my dragon can't go."

"He can go there, as long as he's not in the Void." Martin hung up.

Amber returned her phone to her pocket, stepping into the room. She stood in front of Stanley, sensing Kade and Ronan at her back. After a moment she removed his gag, pulling away the grey duct tape that had been used.

"I still won't tell you anything." Stanley glared up at her.

"I didn't think you would. I just wanted you to know that your loyalty is misplaced."

"We never negotiate with dragons."

"Never?" Amber laughed, a humourless sound. "Yeah, right."

"We don't."

"They didn't have to. Not when they rescued Wayne and," she paused, "What is his name?"

"I still won't tell you anything."

"Okay." She turned her back on him and walked towards Kade and Ronan, who were just inside the room, one on each side of the doorway.

"What are you doing?" Stanley demanded.

Amber looked over her shoulder. "If you won't talk, there's no point in me being here, is there?"

"What are you going to do with me?"

She could smell the fear on him even though he kept it out of his voice. Holding his gaze, she let the silence stretch out. "I don't know." Her words were soft and she held his gaze a moment longer before she turned and left the room. Behind her she heard the door close and then she could no longer sense Stanley.

Once they were back at the water garden, Kade asked, "What are we going to do with him?"

Amber shrugged.

"The Knights don't want him and if we let him go, they'll think he's a traitor. It'd be kinder to kill him," Ronan said.

"Why don't we see what happens after tomorrow?" Amber asked.

"You're not planning on keeping him, are you?" Ronan demanded.

Amber shook her head. "I'd never be able to trust him. I also don't think he'd ever be able to trust us."

"Good."

That wasn't the word that came to her mind, but she decided it was best not to point that out to Ronan or she'd never get to bed. It was probably nearly midnight as it was. "I'll let you know when Martin tells me the location."

"Ring your Knights. Ask them where it's likely to be. Tell them the details we have."

Amber hesitated. It was late, but she guessed Ronan was right. Maybe they'd know. She rang Isaac, waiting for him to answer.

"Is something wrong?"

"No." She explained what Martin had told her. There was silence on the other end. "Do you know where he's likely to suggest?"

"Yeah. No one can remain in the Void there. Your plan won't work. As soon as you step into the area, you'll be forced from the Void. The Knights added sculptures and other things, made from a particular rock, to the park so we'd have a public area that dragons can't use. There's one in every capital city of Australia."

"Ask him how close a dragon can fly to the area," Kade said.

When Amber did, Isaac said, "That might work. You'd have to check it out though because I don't know how far off the ground it goes." He gave her an address.

"Thanks. I'll let you know the results."

"Text them to me. I'm heading to bed," Isaac said.

"Okay. See you tomorrow."

"If your plan works."

She hung up, sliding her phone back into her pocket. "So, can either of you take me to that location?" She smiled when only Ronan nodded. "I should have known."

"When you've lived as long as I have, there are few places you haven't visited."

"You need to fly over it."

Ronan nodded, becoming a dragon.

Kade reached for her, tugging her back to him when she started to climb onto Ronan. "Be careful.

Sometimes when a dragon is forced out of the Void they're also forced into human form."

"Okay." She kissed him, pulling away at the snort Ronan gave. "I'll meet you at the castle when we're done."

With a nod, Kade disappeared into the Void.

Amber clambered onto Ronan's back, glad she had the ability to turn into a goshawk if she should fall. It was much easier to ride a dragon with a saddle. Her legs tightened when he launched into the air, travelling to their destination through the Void, staying in it when they arrived.

Ronan circled lower, shuddering upwards so that Amber was forced to cling tightly or she would have fallen off. *"We can't go any lower than this."*

Amber looked at the ground, wishing someone was there talking to give her a better idea of what it was possible to hear this far from the ground. *"Everyone should be able to hear, shouldn't they?"*

"Yes. As long as he doesn't whisper."

"I guess I'll have to make sure he stays annoyed at me so he doesn't."

"That shouldn't be difficult for you." Ronan took them through the Void.

Amber laughed as they landed in the courtyard of

Temolae Keep. She clambered off him. "Let's hope not."

Turning human, Ronan took hold of her arm and transported her through the Void to her bedroom. "Let me know the moment Martin contacts you."

Amber nodded, sending a text to Isaac once Ronan had left. Then she sent one to her grandfather to let him know she was meeting with Martin some time in the morning. Neither replied. About to search for Kade, she smiled when he stepped out of the Void in front of her.

"What's the verdict?"

"Possible, as long as he doesn't go whispering."

Kade chuckled. "I doubt he'll be in much of a mood for whispering after he's spent a few minutes in your company."

She made a face at him. "Anyone would think I was the most annoying person in the world the way you're going on. You and Ronan."

Still smiling, Kade wrapped his arms around her. "Must be time for bed."

Amber wasn't going to argue that. There was a lot to deal with tomorrow. Meeting Martin in the morning and creating mages in the evening. But only one Knight Mage. She'd hoped for some more. One probably wouldn't be enough. She thought of the hand drawn pictures. No, one definitely wasn't going to be anywhere near enough.

Chapter Seventeen

The morning was nearly half over when Martin finally sent Amber a text telling her where to meet him. She stared at her phone, relieved Isaac had been correct about the location. Especially since they only had an hour to get organised. She sent messages to Ronan, Isaac and Charles, turning to Kade with a grin. Ronan had shown him the pathways to their destination earlier that morning.

"Time to go?"

She nodded. "We have an hour. Finally." She grabbed the long sleeve shirt she'd thrown on the bed earlier that morning in preparation for this moment. Pulling on the shirt to hide her wrist sheaths, she then unbuckled her sword and left it by the bed. She turned to Kade who'd finished removing his own sword. "Ready?"

He nodded. Taking her hand, he entered the Void

and took them to Ronan's water garden. Ronan had told them earlier that morning that he wanted them all to meet there. Kade continued to hold her hand even after they'd arrived.

Amber sighed when she saw Ronan and Charles arguing, Helen occasionally adding her own comment. "Of course no one will be brought out of the Void unless they ask the Gold they're riding to bring them out. We really want to avoid that since it's a public area."

"Then what are you expecting us to do?" Charles asked.

"Witness," Kade said.

Golds brought Isaac, Amos and Eliza out of the Void and Charles demanded, "What are you doing here? Did he convince you to join the dragons?" Charles gestured towards Ronan.

Isaac shook his head, waving Amos back when he started forward. "Amber asked me here. I don't believe a High Protector would be doing anything against the Knights. I thought it best Martin had as many of his own people there to witness the failure of this plan."

Amber was glad Isaac had warned her earlier that morning about the excuse he was using. He sounded so sincere. Doubt hit her and she wondered if maybe he did really believe what he'd said, even after all the proof he'd seen.

"Finally, someone speaking sense." Charles glanced around at the gathered crowd. "Well, are we going to get on with this?"

Once the Golds had changed into their dragon form and were saddled, everyone mounted up and headed through the Void, leaving only Ronan, Amber and Kade on the rooftop garden.

"Don't take any chances, kitten. If you think it's too dangerous, get out of there. And make sure you stay aware of everything. Use all your senses."

"Okay."

Ronan gave her a hard look. "You better be taking this seriously. Don't forget they nearly killed you at Eliza's house."

"I said okay. What more do you want me to say?" Did he have to go on? She was already worried about what might be waiting for her. "I don't need anyone to point out all the dangers. I can figure them out for myself."

"You better. I'll watch you from the unprotected area just outside the park. Call if you need help."

She started to say okay again then decided it probably wasn't the best choice of words. "I will."

Ronan's eyes narrowed.

Amber felt like demanding what did he want her to say. "We have to go. I don't want to be late." She held Ronan's gaze until he nodded, then turned to Kade, taking his hand.

They came out in the park under the deep shadows of a widespread tree that was surrounded by a garden bed filled with ferns and palms. Amber pushed a palm frond aside as they made their way through the garden bed. She searched the area, surprised to find Wayne and the other man in the distance. Next she located Ronan and Martin, crossing the park so she could come from an angle that would put Martin between her and Wayne. If they had a weapon pointed at her, Martin could be her shield.

"Make sure you stand directly behind me. Wayne and the other man who escaped are here," Amber told Kade.

"We don't have to stay here."

"I'll keep Martin between them and us."

"What if there are others?"

"I don't know." She searched the area again. "There's not many people around and none of them are staying still like those three are." She continued to walk towards Martin who stood in the open.

"Anything goes wrong and I'm taking you out of here."

Amber glanced towards him. He was already behind her. She spoke directly to him, worried they were getting close enough for Martin to hear the conversation. *"Maybe you'd be better off taking Martin out of here. I'll fly to Ronan. That's only if we haven't got anything out of him."*

"And if we have got something out of him?"

"I don't know." She fell silent as she stopped in front of Martin. "If your people shoot me, mine will shoot you."

"I don't know what you're talking about."

"Wayne and his friend."

"I haven't seen Wayne in ages. Not since he attacked you."

Amber slowly shook her head. "I know he's been back to the headquarters. I've got surveillance footage of him, Stanley and another man entering the building." She didn't, but he wasn't to know that. "Five days ago." She noticed the flicker of unease in his eyes.

"What do you want?"

Amber stepped slightly to the left. "Ring Wayne and tell him not to move. You really don't want to see what happens if you attack us."

Martin stared at her a moment before he pulled out his phone and dialled a number.

She heard Wayne answer and ordered, "Put it on speaker."

"Martin? You there?" Wayne asked when the phone was on speaker.

"Wayne, I want you and your friend to stay right where you are," Amber said.

"Amber," Wayne snarled.

Amber smiled. "Nice to speak to you too, Wayne. I'm sorry you weren't happy with our accommodations." She sensed him move. "Stay still. I know when you're moving."

"You will pay for this. And for Vikki," Wayne warned.

"Tell your friend to stay still too. I know you're both there." She tracked the man as he moved rapidly away from Wayne. "Immediately, Wayne."

"Get back here." Wayne paused. "Jonah! Back here. She's tracking us."

Amber waited until they were next to each other. "Good. Now stay there until we're finished."

"Martin? What do you want?" Wayne asked.

"Stay there." Martin disconnected the call, returning his phone to his pocket. "What do you want?"

Amber checked the area again before she spoke. "Why are you working for the Knight Mages?"

"I have only ever worked for the Knights."

"Don't give me that rubbish. There's no one in this park but us. So quit with the lies." The Golds flying above her technically weren't in the park. They were above it. "Did you want to check me for listening devices? Is that the problem?"

"We want a pure Gold. Two million dollars if you can get us a pure Gold," Martin said.

She couldn't even imagine that kind of money. It was a ridiculous amount. As bad as offering to pay her weight in gold to an assassin. "You just finished telling me you don't work for the Knight Mages and now you're trying to buy a Gold for them."

"You have no idea what the Knights really protect you against."

"Hell Hounds."

"Wayne said you knew about them, but you don't really know what they are. You've never faced them. Knights have been protecting humans from them for centuries. Long before the Middle Ages."

"Then why don't all the Knights know about them?"

"Because some of them think we'd be better off facing them. We wouldn't. They're nearly impossible to kill. Even you wouldn't be able to face one. They inspire terror. It's like they exude it and those facing them can't help feeling an overwhelming sense of terror and an urge to run. It's nearly impossible to fight against that as well as actually fight the Hounds."

Amber doubted even that would stop her. She'd been terrified plenty of times and still kept going. "So you've hidden your true reason for existence from the Knights."

"No, not our true reason. It's always been to protect humans. Always. That includes from dragons. But we also need dragons."

"For the binding," Amber said.

Martin nodded. "Where did you get your information from?"

"How did you hide all this from most of the Knights? And how do you recruit new Knight Mages?" She breathed in, smelling only dragon bone on him, not the slightly different scent the bone became when someone was a Knight Mage. "And why aren't you one? Aren't you important enough?"

"Do you really think I'm about to tell you all our secrets?"

Amber smiled, mimicking Ronan's smile. She nearly laughed at the wary look that came into Martin's eyes. "You want me to give you our secrets. Answer one of mine and I'll give you an answer too. How did you hide all this from the rest of the Knights?"

Martin stared at her for a moment. "You will tell me how you learned your information. Wayne and Jonah said they told you nothing. And I know Stanley knows nothing of importance."

"I will. As soon as you answer my question."

Again Martin stared at her before he finally spoke. "Knight Mages usually run headquarters. Including those of us who aren't yet full Knight Mages. Sometimes others manage to become the High Protector, but usually we replace them with one of ours fairly quickly. We lost Queensland for a long time, but managed to take it back when Charles was kidnapped. Western Australia recently fell out of our hands, but we'll get it back. We had thought maybe your grandfather would be worth recruiting, but those years of captivity obviously ruined him. And after all the effort we'd put into grooming him before he was caught. We're also working on taking back New South Wales. The Knights usually follow orders blindly. They've sworn to follow their High Protector. Very few ask questions and those that do usually don't last long."

"You kill them?" Amber demanded.

"Don't sound so shocked. How many people have

you killed now? Or other than Vikki has it only been dragons?" He paused. "You owe me an answer."

"Charles said to capture Martin. Answer the question and then fly out of there at the same time as Kade takes Martin through the Void to my water garden," Ronan said to Amber and Kade.

"Grab him at the next word he speaks after I answer him," Amber told Kade before she spoke aloud. "One of my dragons found the information in an old book written by a dragon centuries ago."

"Who-" Martin's words were cut off by Kade grabbing him as Amber flew up into the air, her long sleeve shirt falling away from her to land on the ground.

As she headed for Ronan, she sensed Kade and Martin disappear into the Void while Wayne and Jonah ran across the park towards her. Ronan grabbed hold of her, taking her through the Void to arrive at his water garden, everyone else already there. The moment Ronan let her go, Amber became human again.

Kade and Chait held onto Martin who struggled to escape, threatening to kill them. Amos and Charles yelled at Martin, demanding to know who he'd had killed while Eliza threatened to slit his throat.

"Chait, put Martin in the room with Stanley.

Remove any devices off him that might show his whereabouts," Ronan ordered. "Anrai, help him." He turned to Amber. "I need you to track Wayne and Jonah."

Amber nodded.

Kade grabbed hold of her arm when she took a step towards Ronan. "Not without help."

Ronan crossed the distance between him and Amber, taking hold of her other arm. "I'm not about to get her killed."

"You're not leaving us behind," Amos said, echoed by Charles and Eliza.

"I'm not planning to capture them on my own. We're only going to follow them. When we find out where they're going, then I'll organise enough people to capture them," Ronan said.

"Then you get us," Amos said.

Ronan didn't even bother looking towards Amos, he continued to hold Kade's gaze until Kade let go of Amber's arm.

"Be careful," Kade said directly to Amber.

She didn't know if he would've said more as Ronan took her through the Void to arrive under the tree her and Kade had appeared under earlier. She searched for Wayne and Jonah. "That way." She pointed in their direction.

"How far?"

Amber shrugged, wishing he'd brought the referdex. "I don't know, maybe half of one of those maps out of the referdex we used last time."

Ronan took her through the Void, coming out in the shadows at the side of a derelict building. "Now where?"

Chapter Eighteen

As soon as Amber found them, she pointed in their direction. "That way. About three streets over."

Ronan took them closer, jumping them across the city until Amber lost Wayne and Jonah. "I think they entered a house that I can't search inside of." She frowned, doing a slow circle as she checked out the area. Reaching towards Kade's direction, she tried to figure out how far away Wayne and Jonah had been when they'd disappeared. "I think it's the house they kept me in when they kidnapped me."

"Take me to the house."

"I can't. I don't know exactly where it is. But it's at least four or five streets that way." She pointed in the direction.

Ronan took her through the Void, bringing her out in an overgrown backyard. "Now where?"

Amber started searching the area, eventually

finding a location she couldn't search inside of. "Come on, this way. It's not far." She headed for the front yard, opening up the wooden gate to step onto the footpath.

"Stop running towards danger all the time." Ronan grabbed her arm and took her into the Void, remaining in the street.

"I can't sense the house from here." She hated trying to force her way through the heavier air of the Void.

"Better than being out in the open. When we get closer to where you think it is, we'll take shelter and I'll bring you out of the Void."

It took them nearly half an hour before they found the right house. Amber had also needed to reply to several text messages, reassuring Kade that she was okay and telling Charles they were still tracking Wayne and Jonah. Ronan left her behind the house, hidden against a garden shed near the back fence, while he returned to his water garden. He would need to bring the other Golds through the Void since it would be doubtful that they'd know the pathway to this exact location.

Amber peered around the edge of the shed, wishing she could search inside the house. Who knew how many others were in there with Wayne and Jonah. She felt a gun pressed against the back of her head at the same moment as she sensed Jonah and a Pliethin come out of the Void behind her.

"Inside," Jonah ordered.

Amber walked towards the back door of the house. Where was Ronan? What was taking him so long? She tried to remain calm. Surely help wasn't that far away. "What are you planning to do with me?"

"Shut up and walk."

There was no way she wanted to step inside that house. Anything could be waiting for her on the other side of the door. She couldn't help thinking of the chains in the room downstairs. That wasn't going to happen. No way.

"Open the door."

Mentally searching, she couldn't find Kade, but hoped that someone was still at Ronan's water garden. Reaching for the door, she changed into a goshawk, flying around Jonah to land behind him as a human. Sliding her arm around his chest, she plunged her fingers into the cage, touching the Pliethin. Taking them to Ronan's water garden, she struggled to hold onto Jonah when they arrived. It didn't take him long to throw her off.

She landed on the ground, jumping to her feet as Isaac and Eliza attacked him. Reaching for the chain, she yanked the Pliethin from him as he reached for it. Next, she grabbed Jonah's gun, which had landed on the ground, pointing it at him. "Stop."

"You're a kid. I doubt you've got it in you to pull the trigger."

Ronan stepped out of the Void, glancing towards Amber. "Can't you ever follow orders?" He turned towards Jonah. "And she certainly has it in her to pull the trigger. Don't let her age fool you. She's every inch a warrior."

"You won't get away with this," Jonah said.

Ronan chuckled, grabbing hold of Jonah and pulling him away from Isaac and Eliza before he disappeared into the Void. She lowered the gun, sensing Ronan come out near the room Stanley was kept in, just as her phone rang. Seeing it was Kade, she answered. "I'm safe."

"Where are you?"

"Ronan's house. "

Kade came out of the Void not far from her, hanging up his phone. "What did you think you were doing?" He gestured towards the Pliethin. "Where did you get that from?"

"Jonah. And I didn't exactly plan to come here. It just happened. Well, I chose this place, but I hadn't planned on coming here."

Ronan returned to the water garden. "What did you think you were doing taking on Jonah on your own?"

"Don't you start too. Jonah came out of the Void and held a gun on me," Amber said.

"Where's Amos?" Eliza demanded.

"Trying to kill Wayne while Chait is trying to stop him," Kade said.

"You could have flown out of there," Ronan said to Amber.

She looked around at everyone. Eliza was trying to order Kade to fetch Amos, Ronan glared at her and Isaac slowly shook his head. With how hungry she was getting, it had to be after lunch and she wanted to eat sooner rather than later. "I'll get Amos." Before anyone could argue, she dropped the gun onto the ground and plunged her fingers into the cage, stepping into the Void. She pulled the pathway to her that would take her back to Wayne's house. The back door was open and the sounds of arguing voices drifted out into the yard.

Kade and Ronan appeared beside her. She started to move forward, but Ronan grabbed her arm, pulling her back to him. "I don't want you travelling through the Void by yourself until you know what you're doing."

"I can find my way to your place so I must know what I'm doing." Not that she'd really known if she could manage it on her own, but it had been better than being attacked by Jonah or letting him escape.

Ronan continued to hold Amber's gaze. "Kade, take Amos back to my place. Tell Chait to take Wayne. Then return for Charles and Helen."

"Amber? Will you be okay?" Kade asked her.

"Yeah. Take Amos back to his sister. It might stop her complaining." Although she doubted it. Eliza was sure to find some other problem and blame it on her.

When they were alone, Ronan demanded, "Why do you have to always try and get yourself killed?"

Amber pulled away from his grip. "I don't try and I wasn't even close to getting killed this time."

"Someone had a gun on you. And you don't think that's close to getting killed?"

Her anger faded and she grinned. "Nope. Guess that makes me as crazy as you."

"There isn't always going to be someone there to save you."

She raised her chin, her grin replaced by a glare. "I didn't need anyone to save me. I had it all under control. I even captured Jonah for us."

Ronan held her gaze for several minutes before

he spoke. "Flinn isn't welcome at the warehouse tonight."

"Why not?"

"The less people there to ask awkward questions, the better." He held out his hand. "Do you need help returning to my place?"

She shook her head and pushed her fingers into the cage, taking a step away from him and into the Void. It was becoming easier to enter it, as well as finding the pathways. She came out of the Void in front of Kade, trying to tune out Eliza arguing with Charles. *"What's going on,"* she asked Kade.

"Isaac recorded the conversation you had with Martin and Charles wants a copy. Eliza doesn't want to part with theirs and said that Charles should have thought about recording it himself," Kade said.

Amber faced Isaac. "Send a copy of it to both Charles and me. I'll send you my email address."

"What do you need it for?" Charles demanded.

"What do you need it for?" Amber asked him.

"He wants his old position back," Eliza said. "He doesn't care about who Martin's killed, all he cares about is being High Protector."

"No, I care about not letting anyone else from the Knight Mages take over the Queensland Headquarters."

Amber bit back a sigh as she wondered where Ronan was. He'd probably been sensible enough to stay in the Void rather than come out and deal with this argument. "I got the confession out of Martin. Send me a copy. And send one to my grandfather because we don't know which of the Knights are with the Knight Mages."

Eliza pointed towards Amber. "You could smell which ones are Knight Mages. Don't you reckon you can smell dragon bone on Knights?"

"Martin isn't a Knight Mage. He only works for them. Who's to say the others that work for them are. Only Jonah is one," Amber said.

Ronan came out of the Void with several Golds. "Time for you all to go. I've got things to organise for tonight."

Before they could argue, Charles and Helen were taken into the Void. Isaac grabbed hold of his brother so he couldn't be moved. "Wait."

"What now?" Ronan demanded.

"I've thought about your suggestion." Isaac glanced at each of the Golds before continuing the conversation mentally. *"I want to learn the skills of a Gold dragon."*

"No!" The word burst from Eliza, but she managed

to say the rest mentally. *"Don't even think about it, Isaac."*

"I'll do it. We can't risk your position," Amos said.

"I can't ask it of you," Isaac said.

Amos grinned mirthlessly. *"You didn't. I volunteered."*

"If you're serious, I'll make sure I have a Pliethin there for you," Ronan said.

Amos nodded. *"I'm serious. I'll also want to know how to travel through the Void."*

"It doesn't come immediately," Ronan warned.

"But when it does, I want to know how to do it," Amos said.

Ronan nodded. *"I'm sure there'll be someone willing to teach you."*

"I will," Kade said.

"Why?" Amos asked.

Amber felt like telling him it didn't matter why. He should be grateful Kade was willing to help.

"Because you're currently our ally. Having weak allies weakens us," Kade said.

Amos nodded.

Isaac let go of his brother. "We're ready to leave now."

Amber was relieved when they left without any

more problems. She held out her hand to Kade, threading her fingers through his before turning to Ronan. "I'll see you tonight."

Ronan nodded, vanishing into the Void.

Amber met Kade's gaze. "Want me to take us?"

He chuckled, shaking his head slowly. "Sure."

This time she hardly had to move at all before she slipped into the Void, pulling the correct pathway to herself.

Chapter Nineteen

Jasper cornered Amber while Ronan's Golds were getting everyone ready. They'd already put Amos and Lydia in one of the rooms so no one would know they were there. *"How do we know we can trust that Ronan's been telling us the truth? The Hell Hounds could be something he's made up for some other plan he's got."*

"You're not the only one worried about that." But strangely, she wasn't one of them. *"I'll figure something out so everyone knows it's the truth."*

"He sounds sincere, but then he always does."

"Yeah, but I really think he's telling the truth this time. The complete truth with no hidden motives."

"He's never struck me as the hero out to save the world." Jasper continued to look sceptical.

Amber couldn't blame him. *"He's not. And I don't think that's why he's doing it. He was basically told he was wrong. I think he kind of feels satisfied he was proven right and he'll be the one to come up with the solution."*

"That sounds more like him." Jasper glanced towards Ronan when Anrai brought him a wooden box, the energy of a Pliethin emanating from it. *"I still want to know for sure that this isn't all some cover up for another plan he has."*

"Okay. I'll figure something out." She just wasn't sure how, but she was sure to work it out eventually. She stared at the box Ronan held, guessing there had to be more than one Pliethin with the amount of energy she could sense.

Ronan gestured for them to join him and they crossed the room to stand behind him. Kade and Rian were beside them, Daray and Maira at their backs. Brann had been left at Temolae Keep to watch over it while the rest of them were away. Kade hadn't wanted to leave only Flinn behind. Amber didn't blame him.

Ronan's back was to them, the box with the Pliethins under one arm as he faced the humans waiting to become mages. They stood in rows as Ronan's warriors walked amongst them, blindfolding them. Amber wondered if anyone was dealing with Amos and Lydia. Mentally searching the area around them, she found Hound, one of Ronan's sons with them. There was a Pliethin in there and she guessed Lydia and Amos were about to take its energy. Her attention was dragged back by Ronan speaking.

"I will personally kill any of you who remove your blindfolds." Several people twittered nervously at Ronan's words.

Amber hoped they'd taken her warnings, about upsetting Ronan, seriously. Once everyone was blindfolded, Golds went amongst them pricking fingers and squeezing drops of blood from their fingers into the wounds. Amber held her breath as she watched Alsandair go first to her mother, then Gary. Cooper, Miles and Elliot all stood to the side of Donna and Gary. Amber had been surprised when Miles had come to her earlier and said he wanted to be turned into a proper Dragon Mage. He'd warned her that it didn't mean he'd help her, but she hoped he would. There were so many places she couldn't search inside, like the Knight's headquarters. His talent would be very handy for places like that.

Once everyone had been given Gold Dragon blood, Ronan sent the dragons from the room, including Daray. He turned to face Amber, Kade, Rian and Maira, holding the box of Pliethins out to Rian. He opened the box slightly and Rian slid his hand in, bringing out a Pliethin, a feather in his other hand. She noticed Rian wore gloves.

As Rian moved away, Ronan held the box out to Kade next and then to Maira. Each removed a Pliethin before crossing the room to the blindfolded humans, a goshawk feather in their hands. Ronan brought the box to Amber last, keeping the lid closed as he stood in front of her.

She held his gaze, waiting for him to speak. He remained silent. *"What do you want, Ronan?"*

"You will have two weeks to train the new mages. Don't waste it." Ronan opened the box slightly.

Amber held his gaze as she slid a hand inside, steeling herself against the stinging sensation as she took the Pliethin. It was more powerful than the caged one she had at home. She wanted to argue that two weeks wasn't enough, but could tell from Ronan's hard expression that she'd be wasting her breath. Instead she nodded and strode towards her mother, drawing a feather from her pocket.

Once everyone had held the Pliethins, they returned them to Ronan who put the half worn Pliethins back into the box. He gave the box to Rian who, with a nod, took it and strode towards the room Cooper and Miles had once been held in.

Amber watched him go, hoping he'd be fine. She

remembered the night Kade had held a Pliethin and how he'd been completely unaware of his surroundings. She glanced towards Kade. *"Take care of my family."* At his nod, she hurried after Rian. *"Let me help you."*

About to close the door, Rian opened it further stepping out of the way so she could follow him into the room. "It is not necessary."

Amber smiled. "Isn't that usually my line?" She wished Crystal could have been here for him, but Flinn had complained and Crystal had said that she was sure there was nothing she'd miss out on. It looked like Crystal was wrong.

Rian grinned fleetingly and nodded. "Usually." He closed the door behind them. He handed the box over to her and removed his gloves, dropping them onto the floor. He took one of the Pliethins from the box before he strode to the middle of the small room.

Amber watched as he became a dragon, drawing the energy from the half spent Pliethin. As it lost its glowing energy, she hurried forward with another Pliethin, exchanging it for the spent one. She remembered how Kade had thanked his Pliethin and she did the same before letting it go. The Pliethin vanished from the room.

Once all four Pliethins had been drained, Rian

collapsed forward onto the ground, turning human. Amber knelt in front of him, reaching out to check he was okay.

"I am fine." He brushed her hand away as he struggled to sit.

She eyed him, trying to see any changes. *"Why did you use the half worn Pliethins? Will that make it less likely to work?"*

Rian shook his head. *"It was kinder to drain them so they could more easily return to their own world."*

"How long before we know if this will work?"

Rian shrugged. *"I do not know. I do not know if it will work."*

"How do you feel?" She looked him over again.

An exhausted smile slowly formed. *"Like I could sleep for a week."*

"Is that normal?"

He nodded.

"Then maybe it is working."

"Maybe. But there are several more days of this to be sure it does."

"I know it'll work. Watching you was like watching Kade with the Pliethin. And Flinn."

Rian nodded, struggling to his feet. *"You can return to your family now."* He gestured towards the door.

"Are you coming out?"

"Soon."

Amber stared at him, still unable to see any changes. *"Are you sure you're okay?"*

"Yes. I will be out in a minute."

Amber watched him a moment longer before she nodded and headed for the door. Outside the room, the humans were talking amongst themselves. Her gaze was drawn to her mother who was talking and laughing with Roger, the five humans he'd brought with him nearby. Gary was talking to Miles, who regularly nodded, while Cooper seemed to have appointed himself as Miles' protector and stood beside him.

Angela broke away from her group of friends, hurrying over to Amber. "I don't feel any different. Am I meant to?"

"No, not yet. Give it a bit of time."

"How much time? I mean days? Weeks?"

Amber grinned. "Not that long. By morning you should notice some differences. Possibly sooner." She probably wouldn't have noticed quite so quickly if she hadn't been trying to escape a wyvern.

Angela threw her arms around her, holding her tight. "I keep thinking this is a dream. This is the most amazing thing that has ever happened to me."

"Yeah, I know," Amber said before she spoke directly to Daray who she sensed was headed towards her. *"I'm fine."*

Daray continued to cross the room towards her. *"I will make sure you remain that way."* Amber drew away from Angela, shaking her head a couple of times as she sent a look to Daray who stopped at her shoulder before she turned back to Angela. "You'll have a fortnight to train before things start to get interesting."

"Interesting? I thought things were already interesting," Angela said.

Kade joined them. "She's talking about war."

"I'm talking about Hell Hounds," Amber said.

Kade shrugged. "Same thing."

Angela glanced around. "Where's Crystal?"

"Ronan wouldn't let Flinn be here so Flinn wouldn't let Crystal be here without him," Amber said.

"He owns her?" Angela asked.

"He wishes." Amber glanced towards Rian who came out of the room, closing the door behind him. "Crystal decided it wasn't worth the argument. Not like she doesn't know how it's done, or Flinn for that matter." She shrugged. "But Ronan didn't want too many here." Or people who'd wonder what Rian was up to.

"So when do I get to see your castle?" Angela asked

"Soon. Once we sort out the training schedule and who else is coming to the castle," Amber said.

Rian reached her side. "I will take care of that if you wish to leave now."

Amber nodded. "I have to talk to my mum first." She crossed the room, Daray at her shoulder, leaving Kade and Rian with Angela. She came to a stop beside her mother, waiting for her to finish speaking to Roger. "We're headed back to the castle, did you want to come?" Amber glanced towards Roger. "You're welcome to visit if you want."

"Thank you," Roger said. "I've invited Donna to stay with me for a couple of weeks so we can get to know each other again."

Amber started to protest. Before she had a chance, Daray spoke. "She needs to meet her Gold Warrior and get to know her warrior before she spends time visiting you."

"I'm not about to be a warrior or fighter or anything like that," Donna said.

"It's all about protection and learning self defence," Daray said.

Gary joined them. "That is the most logical

decision. It is after all why we chose to become Dragon Mages in the first place." He turned to Roger with a smile. "I'm sure even you will be spending a lot of time over the next couple of weeks becoming accustomed to your new skills."

Roger nodded. "Yes of course. I hadn't thought of that." He smiled ruefully. "It's taken so long to be released from my promise that I was being impatient. I'm sure there'll be plenty of time to get to know each other again."

Goodbyes were soon made and Amber and Kade returned to Temolae Keep with Angela and her friends. Donna and Gary chose to return to their own place and Rian remained behind to organise training schedules. Amber had no idea what Ronan planned to do since he left before everyone else, telling no one of his plans.

Back at the castle, Amber had one of the servants show everyone around while several more prepared rooms. Amber and Kade retreated to their own room where Amber's gaze was drawn to the two Pliethins hanging on the curtain rod. One on either side of the window.

"We should see if Maira and Brann can use the Pliethins to travel through the Void."

Kade nodded "I was thinking about suggesting that

when we had a spare moment." He grinned. "Things haven't stopped being crazy since you returned, so I doubt we'll find one."

"That's not my fault. You dragons and the Knights are the ones who cause all the craziness."

"Yeah, but you were nearly a Knight. Maybe crazy was already in your genes."

She crossed the room to slide her arms around his waist, meeting his gaze. "I'm glad I'm not."

Kade wrapped his arms around her, holding her close. "I'm glad too." His lips met hers as his arms tightened around her.

Chapter Twenty

The next two weeks passed quickly. As they approached the end of the time Ronan had allowed them, Amber worried the mages wouldn't be ready. Even she had been given a lot more than two weeks to prepare for her first battle. Angela and her friends remained at the castle and Crystal convinced Flinn to help train them. Amber was surprised before the two weeks ended that somehow Flinn agreed to have Angela for his mage instead of Crystal. He seemed to get along a lot better with her than he had with Crystal. Even though she was worried about how Angela would cope with Flinn, she was glad that Crystal would have Rian for her Gold Warrior.

When Rian had told her that the experiment had worked, she'd grinned. "I guess this means you'll finally have to stop being my first warrior."

"We will see."

She had laughed, not really having expected any other answer.

Amber had suggested to Kade that they use the same technique for Maira and Brann.

Kade had shaken his head "We'd have no way to explain it and once everyone figured out how it was done, not a single Gold would be safe. Every warrior would be hunting them down for their hearts."

That was the last thing she wanted. The life of a Gold Warrior was dangerous enough without that.

Charles had taken over as High Protector of the Brisbane headquarters and Roy had returned to the headquarters, but kept in touch with Amber. He told her there was fighting and distrust amongst all the Knights, since they had seen the recording, including the ones overseas.

The evening before the two weeks were up, Amber sensed Ronan arrive in the planning room. Letting Kade know, she used the Pliethin she'd taken to hanging at her belt, to travel through the Void to the planning room. Kade stepped out of the Void and into the planning room to stand beside her.

Ronan was seated on the edge of the table, waiting for them. "Not bad timing. Are you able to respond as quickly to anyone who enters the castle, or is it only to those you have ties to."

"Anyone." Rian had been making her practice, but she wasn't about to tell Ronan that. He'd probably somehow see the accomplishment as all due to him. "Are you here to talk about attacking the Knight Mages?"

"Something like that."

"Exactly why are you here then?"

"I need you to come and have a look at something with me." Ronan stepped away from the table.

Kade took hold of Amber's hand. *"You don't have to go with him."*

"I know." Her gaze remained on Ronan. "Is this to do with the Hell Hounds?"

"Yes."

She turned to Kade with a smile. *"I'll be fine. He's not about to get me killed."*

Kade drew her close, kissing her before he let her go. *"Get out of there if you run into trouble."* His gaze momentarily dropped to the Pliethin. *"Don't stick around if it's more than you can handle."*

Letting go of him, Amber nodded before she turned to Ronan, holding out her hand. He took it, taking them to his family crypt before letting her hand go. "This doesn't look like anything to do with the Hell Hounds."

"Learn this pathway. It's a safe location. More safe

than your planning room. But be quick about it because you can't remain in the Void in here so the moment you enter it, you'll be thrown out of it if you don't immediately shift elsewhere."

"Where do you want me to shift to?"

"Back out of the Void. It's less painful coming out of the Void yourself than to be thrown out of it."

Amber nodded, pressing her fingers against her Pliethin before she entered the Void, stepping straight back out of it as she fought against being pushed from it. "Well that wasn't pleasant."

"It wasn't meant to be." Ronan held out his hand to her again.

She didn't take it. "Why?"

"You're going to have to explain yourself a little better than that if you're expecting an answer."

"Why do you want me to have access to the crypt?"

Ronan held her gaze for nearly a minute. "You're not the only one who will have access."

"Who else?"

"Rian."

"What about Kade?"

"You're not to show anyone else the pathway to here. I will kill them, no matter who they are to you. You bring them here and you're asking me to kill them. Understand?"

She could tell by the tone of his voice exactly how serious he was. "Yes." She relaxed slightly when the hard look left his eyes. "Was this all you wanted to show me?"

"No." Ronan took hold of her hand, taking her through the Void again. They came out in a shallow gully partway up a rocky hillside.

Amber automatically searched for Kade. "We're in a different country?"

"Quiet."

"Are we? In a different country?"

"Yes."

"What are we doing here?"

"This is as close as we can get to where the binding is done. I need you to see if you can find out how many are guarding the place."

"Where are we?"

"Can you focus for once? They regularly patrol this area, at random intervals. Now can you tell me who is around here?"

"Not if they're in the Void. You should have brought Crystal."

"Amber."

She could almost hear the growl in his thoughts. *"Okay. Fine. Give me a minute."* She'd been mentally searching the area ever since they'd arrived, but now she tried a more focused search. She couldn't get any better results. It was like they were the only ones here. Throughout the area she found blank spaces, which she guessed were areas protected from her ability to search. As well as numerous little pockets, there was one large area. Even her better than average ability to see in the dark didn't show any more than her mental search had shown. *"There are too many blank spots I can't search."*

"You need to convince Miles to have a look. Otherwise, we're going in there blind."

"I'll try."

"Do you want to take Kade, Crystal and Rian in there without knowing what they're going to face?"

"Of course not. I already said I'd try."

"Don't try. Convince."

Before Amber could say anything else, Ronan took her through the Void to the planning room at Temolae keep. Kade and Rian were sitting at the table, obviously waiting for her. She turned to Ronan with a glare, grabbing hold of his hand when he let go. "Stop doing that."

"Call me as soon as he agrees. No matter the hour." Ronan tugged away from her grip and disappeared.

Amber growled, staring at the spot where he'd been. "Bloody dragons."

Rising to his feet, Kade chuckled. "I guess there wasn't too much danger wherever he took you. Not with the mood you're in."

"No. Not really." She frowned. "At least I guess not. He took me near where the binding has been done."

"You don't think that was dangerous?" Kade slowly shook his head. "No wonder I worry about you."

"There was no need to. I was fine." Amber suddenly realised that even though Ronan had given her a chance to learn the pathway to his crypt, he hadn't given her a chance to learn the one to where the binding was done. Her gaze narrowed. It was the first thing she was going to do the next time she returned there, regardless of what he wanted. There was no point in being able to walk the Void if she had no pathways to travel. She headed for the door.

"Where are you going?" Kade asked

"To talk to Miles." She flung open the door and stepped into the hallway since she found it difficult to enter the Void from the planning room. Finally locating Miles, she used the Void to bring herself to his room, where he was lying on the bed reading. He jumped to his feet, his book falling to the floor, his hands raised as if to attack.

When his gaze focused on her, he lowered his hands. "What do you want?"

"Your help."

"Are my choices help or be kicked out?"

Amber shook her head. "No, nothing like that." She held his gaze a moment before she continued to speak "I won't lie to you. It's a dangerous area we need to search, but if you help we'll have a better idea of what we have to face and can prepare for it. It will improve our chances of survival."

"If I don't and someone dies, are you saying it'll be my fault?"

She wanted to say yes, but instead she shook her head. She sensed Cooper walking down the hallway before he entered the room. "Did you want something?"

Cooper looked between Amber and Miles, an uncomfortable expression on his face.

Amber shook her head, turning to Miles. "You didn't have to call him. I'm not about to force you."

"What's going on?" Cooper asked.

Amber explained what she'd already said to Miles.

Cooper swallowed visibly. "I'll go with you when you attack there."

"I thought you'd be on my side," Miles said.

"I am, but that also means we need to be on Amber's side. She's the only one who's tried to protect us," Cooper said.

"I just want to be left alone." Miles sat heavily on the edge of his bed, dropping his head into his hands. "Completely alone."

She knew that feeling. Had once thought that was what she'd wanted. "I'm sorry, but I had to ask you. Had to see if you'd help us out. I didn't want to take my people in there blindly without first making certain you couldn't help." She turned away, headed for the door, not sure that she'd be able to travel through the Void with the disappointment and worry she battled.

"Where are you going?" Miles asked.

She stopped, her hand on the doorhandle, and looked over her shoulder. "Leaving you alone."

"But–" Miles frowned, rising to his feet, glancing towards Cooper. "I mean–"

She waited, but he remained silent. "Spit it out, Miles. I don't have all night."

"That's it? You're not going to make me?"

Letting go of the handle, she turned to face him. "Is that what you want? Someone to tell you what you have to do? Because that's not me. I want you to help.

I would like you to tell me what we'll face when we go in there. But that has to be your choice. You have to want to be there, have to be willing to take the risk and fight at my side if something goes wrong. Otherwise, you're useless to me." When he continued to stand there, staring at her, she guessed he was out of questions. "Goodnight." Again she turned away, this time getting the door open before he spoke.

"I'll do it."

She faced him. "What?"

"I'll do it."

"You'll go with us and search the area."

He nodded.

"Now." At least she guessed Ronan would want to go immediately. Otherwise why would he have asked to know the moment Miles agreed?

Fear crossed his face and he glanced towards Cooper before meeting Amber's gaze. "Right this minute?"

"Not quite. Half an hour or so. As soon as everyone is ready."

Miles swallowed visibly. "Okay."

"I'll let Ronan know." She held his gaze a moment longer, giving him a chance to change his mind. When he remained silent, she stepped into the hallway, heading for her room, ringing Ronan as she walked.

"That was quick, even for you."

Amber laughed at his greeting.

"What did you threaten him with?"

"I doubt you'd believe me." She hung up the phone when she sensed Ronan appear in the planning room. Pushing her fingers into the cage, she focused on travelling there through the Void. She still couldn't manage without entering the Void first.

"Try me," Ronan said when she appeared in front of him.

"Well, I suppose you could say I threatened him with leaving him alone."

"Solitary confinement?"

Grinning, she shook her head. "He wanted to be left alone, so I agreed. He changed his mind."

"I doubt you humans will ever make sense to me."

"That's not surprising since we don't make sense to ourselves half the time." She paused. "Who are we taking with us?"

"Rian, Crystal since he wasn't willing to leave her behind, and probably Kade since you're likely to be difficult about leaving him behind and Miles."

Amber nodded. "Cooper wants to go too."

"It's not a sight seeing expedition."

"I know. But if Cooper wants to go and keep an eye on Miles, then he goes too."

"I'm trying to keep the group small so that hopefully we aren't noticed."

"What if they spot us and there are too many people there for us to handle?"

"We get out of there and come back with an army."

She hesitated, not sure she really wanted to know the answer. "And what happens if we find out there's only a small amount of people there?"

"We take them and the place."

Her heart felt like it skipped a beat and she fought to keep her expression neutral. "You said we had two weeks. It's not Saturday yet."

"Do you want to wait the half hour until it is?"

"No." She could do this. Hadn't she survived numerous battles already? "Let's get organised then."

"I'll take Rian then Crystal there and be back for the rest of you. Have them ready and waiting here for me."

Ronan disappeared into the Void before she could speak and she sensed him appear near Rian and Crystal before disappearing with Rian. She sighed. He hadn't given her much time.

She soon found it was enough. Cooper and Miles

stepped into the planning room just before Ronan returned from taking Crystal, Kade having come straight to her when she'd called him. Cooper insisted he'd go before Miles and Amber went last, not wanting to chance Ronan leaving anyone behind. As soon as she arrived, she entered the Void and came straight back out again.

Chapter Twenty-One

"What do you think you're doing?" Ronan asked.

Amber grinned when she saw Kade and Rian do the same. "Learning the pathway." She held his gaze, her chin rising when he glared at her.

"There's no one in the Void around here," Crystal said, then grinned. "Well, not now anyway."

Amber bit back a laugh when she met Crystal's gaze.

"Do you still want me to search the area?" Miles kept looking around as if expecting something to jump out at him.

"Yeah," Amber said.

"I'll make sure you're safe while you're gone," Cooper said.

Miles nodded, sitting on the ground. "It makes it easier." He was silent for several minutes. "I'm above you now. You do know that I can't see if anyone is in the Void, don't you?" His voice had a hollow sound to it.

"Just tell us what you can see." Amber tried to keep the impatience from her voice. She wasn't sure if she completely succeeded.

"I'm entering a building. Well, it's actually a building built inside the hill. Maybe it's a cave carved out to look like a building."

"This isn't an architectural show. Tell me about people and defences only," Ronan growled.

"I can see four people. Once you enter the building, or the cave, there is a long tunnel before you reach the main room where they are. There are two side rooms, but no one is in them. A bunk room and a kitchen with a bathroom off it. That's it," Miles said.

"What's in the main room?" Ronan asked.

"I thought you didn't want me to describe the place," Miles said.

"That didn't stop you from telling me there was a kitchen. Now tell me what's in the main room," Ronan ordered.

"A big rock thing. A bit like a bird bath, but bigger and deeper and chunkier looking. Not a sculpture, but it's all carved like it's some kind of decoration. It's right in the middle of the room."

"Are you sure there are only four people in there?" Rian asked.

"No. There might be people in the Void," Miles said.

"Can you tell if it would be impossible to stay in the Void?" Amber asked.

"No."

"We're going in. You stay in that area and let us know if any of them move or if more arrive." Ronan turned to Cooper. "Help him up."

"But we're not armed," Cooper said.

"Did someone cut off your hands?" Ronan demanded.

Cooper shrank back from him. "N… no."

Amber stepped between them. "Leave him alone." She held Ronan's gaze for a moment before she turned to Cooper. "All you have to do is protect Miles. If anyone attacks, you ice them. We'll take care of the ones in there. You and Miles keep a look out for any others that might arrive."

Cooper nodded, helping Miles to his feet and keeping an arm around his shoulders.

"We need to go straight ahead and slightly to the left to find the entrance," Miles said. "I think there might be a camera at the entrance."

"You think or you know?" Ronan demanded.

"Uhmm… Possibly?"

"Don't go getting us killed, boy."

"I'll fly ahead." Amber turned into a goshawk and flew in the direction Miles had given them. It didn't take her long to spot the security camera, hidden in the rocks above some large shrubs. She was able to dislodge gravel and pebbles so they fell in front of it. *"It's safe now."* She landed beside the shrubs, turning human. Mentally searching the area, she found they were still alone. She kept track of her companions as they came closer, continually searching the area and wishing she could check the unsearchable space behind her.

"They haven't moved. They're all still in the main room," Miles said.

While she waited for them to reach her side, Amber had a look behind the shrubs. There was a heavy timber door that when she tried to open it she found it was locked. *"I've found a locked door."*

Ronan was the first one to reach her side and had the door open in minutes. *"Are they still in the main room?"*

"Yes," Miles said.

Ronan stepped into the narrow tunnel, Amber directly behind him. She hoped the people stayed in the main room because there wasn't space for fighting in this tunnel. She stayed close behind Ronan, sensing Kade directly behind her. Next was Crystal followed by Rian and well behind him was Miles and Cooper.

As they reached the end of the tunnel, Amber sensed a Pliethin. The four people in the room drew swords as Ronan stepped into the main room, followed by everyone but Cooper and Miles. Seeing one of the men reaching for the caged Pliethin hanging at his neck, she turned into a goshawk, flying across the room. Turning human, she grabbed hold of him, plunging her fingers into the cage of her own Pliethin, fighting to keep him there. It felt like the air was pressing in, trying to crush her.

Then Kade was at her side, wrenching the Pliethin from the man who staggered back from them. He quickly regained his balance and attacked. Amber dropped back, unable to hold her own against the Knight Mage. Ronan joined Kade and Amber glanced around the room. Seeing Crystal and Rian outnumbered, she crossed the short distance between them, attacking the only woman in the room. Like Crystal, she used her mage powers. Then she worried she'd kill the Knight and instead drew one of her daggers and threw it at her, hoping to wound her. The woman dodged, but she was unable to avoid Amber turning into a goshawk and coming up behind her as a human. Amber hit the woman hard on the back of her head with the hilt of her sword, watching her crumple to the ground.

It didn't take them long to subdue the other two Knights and, collecting her dagger, Amber turned towards Kade and Ronan who still fought the Knight Mage. Ronan had him by the throat while Kade had half his body pinned to the wall. Drawing back his sword, Ronan stared into the man's eyes.

Amber flew across the room, landing near Ronan. "Don't kill him. At least not yet."

Ronan's hand remained around the man's throat, his sword still drawn back. "Get out of the way."

"Not until he answers some questions." Then she spoke directly to Ronan. *"I want everyone else to believe you about this."*

"What about you?"

She held his gaze. *"I already believe you."*

Ronan lowered his sword. "If you can't make him talk, he dies."

Rian strode forward with grey metal chains. The Knight Mage fought against wearing them and Amber wondered if they actually worked on them. She knew they didn't work for Dragon Mages. Or at least they certainly hadn't worked on her.

"You're wasting your time. I won't talk." The man stared at her defiantly, his hands cuffed.

Amber gestured towards the carved stone in the middle of the room. It reminded her of a large bowl on a stand. The pedestal-like stand was carved to show Knights, dragons and Hell Hounds fighting. "This won't last."

"You know nothing," the man said.

"I know that you sacrifice dragons to keep three worlds bound together so the Hell Hounds can't come here. And I know that the binding is becoming weaker all the time, never lasting as long," Amber said.

"What did you do to Jonah? We'll kill you for this. Don't think we're the only ones," the man warned.

"Jonah didn't tell us anything."

"We'll find him and take him back. You can't keep him hidden forever."

Ronan laughed. "Are you saying you can find someone who's hidden in the Void?"

"No, but you have to bring him out occasionally. We'll be waiting."

Amber wanted to ask why Ronan was keeping Jonah in the Void and if he kept the other two in there as well, but they didn't have time for that right now. "The binding will fail."

"No. All we have to do is find dragons that are from a pure Gold line," the man said.

"Ariana, the last dragon you used, was from a pure line," Ronan growled. "The binding is failing, like my grandfather told the ones who built it."

"I don't know her name, but she couldn't be. The binding was weak from the very start this time." He glanced towards the kitchen doorway. "We've got photos. You can see for yourself who she was. See that she wasn't pure."

"Trophies?" Amber demanded.

He shook his head. "No, nothing like that. So none were forgotten. Their sacrifices kept us all safe. A memorial. On the wall in the kitchen. Some are drawings, the modern ones were taken by a camera."

Ronan pushed the man towards the doorway. "Show us. And don't even think about trying to escape. I know all I need to. Even to humour my mage I'm not about to let you escape."

Amber sent Ronan a daggered look. He intercepted it with an amused one. *"Don't patronise me, Ronan."*

"I'm not, kitten. But I won't show them weakness or let them think they have something I need," Ronan said directly to Amber.

She stared at the wall when they stepped into the

kitchen. It was covered in pictures. From oldest to newest, starting at the left and travelling down the wall in columns. Hand drawn, painted, photographs. Some were smudged and faded. Rows of black and white photos eventually gave way to colour. The final picture was halfway down the wall. Amber looked into the defiant gold eyes, bronze hair tangled around her face while two hooded figures held her captive.

"That's Ariana." Ronan jabbed his finger at the picture.

Kade stared at the photos. "They're Gold. Many of them pure Gold."

The man shook his head. "Impossible. They can't be."

Ronan slammed him against the wall beside the pictures. "Take a closer look. They're Gold. Most of them the purest of Gold. Their sacrifices were worthless. They gave you a handful of years in exchange for hundreds of their own years."

"It can't be true. The binding can't fail. You don't know what that means if it fails." The man struggled to escape Ronan.

"Then how about you tell me," Ronan said.

"We're dead. All humans are dead. Humans, Knights, Knight Mages. Dead."

"What about the dragons?" Amber asked. "You didn't mention the dragons."

The man met her gaze. "Because they can win against them. They can turn into their dragon form, strike then retreat. Hell Hounds can't fly. They can move fast, but they can't fly."

Before Amber could ask another question, Miles said, *"More are coming. They're running up the hill. We've got maybe a minute. There's fourteen."*

She felt Cooper and Miles move into the main room. A moment of panic hit her. How were they meant to face another fourteen? And how many of them were Knight Mages? They'd barely taken this one. Meeting Ronan's steady gaze, her panic receded.

"Destroy the binding," Ronan said.

Amber nodded, turning into a goshawk and flying into the main room. Behind her she could hear the man screaming that they were making a mistake. She landed in the stone bowl, turning human and drawing her sword. The bowl was as large as a double bed and in the centre was a jagged hole, barely big enough to put her hand into it. Remembering the instructions she'd read in the book Ronan had given her, she called flames to her sword before plunging it into the hole.

"No!" People burst into the main room, a woman with a caged Pliethin screaming at her.

Amber could barely focus on her surroundings. It felt like her entire body was engulfed in flames. She screamed, her head thrown back as the bowl shattered, falling to the ground in large chunks, only her sword keeping her from falling too. She tightened her grip on it as she fought to stay in place.

The flames died down and Amber slumped forward, the jagged hole and the pedestal all that was left of the bowl. Hands grabbed her as she started to fall, Kade pulling her sword from the pedestal. Arguments raged in the background. Guns and swords were drawn and she noticed her people had their backs to her, facing the Knights in front of them, the shackled man now with his own people. It took her a moment to realise that Rian was gone. She drew away from Kade and Crystal, who'd helped her to the ground, and drained power from one of her bracelets before she took her sword.

"Where's Rian?"

"Bringing an army," Ronan said.

"How long until they're here?" the shackled man asked.

Ronan grinned, his predatory one. "You're too late.

Do you think you can do much with this handful? I have an army out there waiting for me."

"They've got to get to you first. No one can enter here through the Void."

Amber automatically searched the area, looking for the army Ronan had mentioned. She couldn't find them, but realised she could now search outside the area they stood in. "I wouldn't be too sure of that. This building has changed since the binding was broken." She frowned. "Actually, there's something odd with the air. Like a wave of something."

"Fear." The shackled man held out his hands. "Let me go. Don't leave me to die chained."

Ronan shook his head. "Do you take me for an idiot? Then what? Give you a knife to stab me with?"

"No. You haven't got a clue what you're about to face. Can't you feel the fear building? By the time they arrive we'll barely be able to fight them. We'll be fighting against our urge to run every bit as hard as we'll be fighting against the Hell Hounds." Continuing to hold out his hands, he took a step towards them, the grey chain rattling at his movements. "Let me go. Please."

Chapter Twenty-Two

Amber pushed past Ronan, sheathing her sword. "What's your name?"

The man stared at her like she'd gone mad. "We don't have time for this. The hounds are coming."

A shiver passed through Amber as she heard the echo of Vikki in his words. "I know. So you better tell me quickly."

"Simon."

Amber took another step closer to him. "Can we trust your word?"

"More than you can trust the word of a dragon."

"What are you doing, kitten?"

She ignored Ronan. "If we let you go to fight against the Hell Hounds, you have to come with us once we defeat them. Not all the Hell Hounds, just the ones that are coming right now."

A woman moved to stand beside Simon and grabbed his arm. "Don't do it."

"Why would you trust me to keep my word?" Simon pulled his arm from her grip.

Amber held his gaze a moment, feeling the sensation of fear slowly increase. "Because we have Jonah and Wayne." She didn't bother mentioning Stanley as he obviously wasn't important to them. "All we want to do for now is talk." And hopefully find a way to call a truce so they could all work towards getting rid of the Hell Hounds.

"What happens if I don't agree?"

"Don't give in to them." Again the woman grabbed Simon's arm.

He shook her off like he had before. "Let go, Hannah." His gaze remained on Amber. "We're running out of time. Can't you feel it?"

"What do you think will happen? If you lie to us, what do you think we'll do to Jonah?" She didn't have a clue what she'd be capable of doing, but doubted it would be anywhere near what Ronan would do.

"If I come with you, will you set Jonah and Wayne free?"

Amber shook her head. "No."

"If you come with us after this battle we will keep you for no more than a week. Providing you don't try to escape and your people don't try to find you," Ronan said.

Simon didn't even glance towards Ronan. He continued to hold Amber's gaze, ignoring the warnings from his own people. Finally, he held out his hands. "I give you my word."

Ronan took a key from his pocket and unlocked the shackles, letting them drop to the ground. Stepping back, he withdrew his phone and made a call. "It's time. Only a handful." He hung up.

"What's going on?" Hannah demanded.

"Reinforcements," Ronan said. "Even I can feel the change in air pressure."

Rian brought Daray into the room for a moment. When Rian let go of him, Daray disappeared. Rian did the same and they both reappeared with Alsandair and Chait.

"Looks like I broke more than just the binding," Amber said.

"How many more are you bringing in here?" Hannah demanded.

"That's enough for now. We need space to fight. We'll see how many hounds come through," Ronan said.

"They must be getting closer." Cooper rubbed his hands up and down his arms.

"Are we just going to stand around here, waiting?" Crystal asked. "Isn't there anything we can do?"

"Practice trying not to run," Hannah said.

She felt a large wave of fear rush over her. Cooper whimpered beside her. It was a familiar sensation. One she'd lived with for months. The exact sensation she felt every time she faced a battle. A smile formed and her shoulders straightened. She was more than ready. This was what drove her. This sensation.

"Can't you feel it?"

She glanced towards Simon, nodding. "Yeah, but this is what makes me fight. Fear for those I need to protect."

Ronan laughed, gesturing towards her. "She is what mages once were. They thrived on the fear the hounds brought, leaving death in their wake."

Amber opened her mouth to argue. Three creatures came out of the Void, each seven foot tall, snarling, with large fangs visible. They looked like upright, rabid dogs with clawed hands and heat emanating from them, waves of terror preceding them.

Cooper shrank back, whimpering again. Amber stepped in front of him and Miles. "You back with us, Miles?"

"Yes." There was fear in his voice.

"Good. Then stay out of the way." She ran towards the closest Hell Hound, who was already under attack from some of her people. The rest helped the Knights fight the other two. Turning into a panther, she launched herself at the hound. They crashed to the ground in a tangle of limbs and she turned into a goshawk, flying away as he tried to crush her. He was on his feet before she landed and became human again. She barely managed to dodge his attack and it was only because the hound also fought Kade and Ronan that he missed her. She had to learn how to move faster.

Becoming a goshawk, she darted in behind him, landing and becoming human as he spun to face her. By the time her daggers were in her hands, flames bursting along the blades, the hound was facing her. She plunged the daggers into his body, one into his stomach, the other in his chest. The smell of burning flesh filled the air around her as she let go of the daggers to again turn into a goshawk and fly out of the crushing grip of the hound.

He roared, clawing at the daggers that were embedded in his body, swatting at the blades that Ronan, Kade and Rian attacked him with. Landing, Amber drew her sword, wondering how much it was going to take to kill the beast. She drew fire to her blade, attacking him with it. He howled, blocking her with his razor sharp claws. When he turned to meet Kade's blade, she plunged her sword into his side. He barely faltered.

"Here!"

Amber turned towards Kade, catching the sword he threw to her, calling flame to his blade as she drove it into the hound. The beast roared, molten blood pouring over her hands as he fell towards her, Kade and Ronan dragging him off her.

She stared down at the beast as she healed the blisters his blood had caused on her hands and arms, taking the weapons Rian had retrieved for her. Looking around, she saw there was still one hound fighting. He was surrounded. Scattered around the room were unmoving bodies. A glance showed that none of them were her people, but she had to look. Had to see if they were alive or could be healed.

Most of them had minor wounds, one was dead, and one looked like he wouldn't last much longer. She tried to heal the man, but the dragon bone still wasn't enough. She called Rian to her. *"I want to give him some dragon blood, but I'm not sure if I should use Gold blood."*

"I will bring Maira."

Rian disappeared before she could say anything.

Pressing her hands against the torn flesh of the man's chest, she tried to slow the bleeding. It didn't help. Her hands were immediately covered in blood.

Rian and Maira came out of the Void and Maira knelt beside her, dripping blood into the Knight's wound. Amber felt the life ebbing away and she frantically tried to knit together the torn flesh. She vaguely heard Simon and Hannah arguing with Rian, while Kade and Ronan kept them from their companion. Drawing power from another bracelet, she continued to try and heal the Knight.

"Maira, more blood, please."

Maira came forward again, dripping more blood onto the man's wound. He opened his eyes to stare up at Amber. His blue eyes were filled with confusion, then panic. He began to fight against her hands, trying to pull away.

"Rian!" Maira called out, pinning one of the man's arms down. Rian knelt at the other side of him to do the same.

"Don't fight me," Amber said softly. "You'll tear open what I've repaired."

"You're poisoning me."

"It is the dragon blood. You will recover from it," Rian said.

"Why?" The man continued to look up at Amber as she crouched over him.

The wound finally closed and she sat back on her heels, drawing power from two of her bracelets. "I'm a healer."

Cooper knelt beside her, a bowl of water held out.

She gratefully rinsed some of the blood from her hands, trying not to focus on the colour of the water. Rian helped her to her feet and she stepped out of the way as the Knights crowded in to check on the man.

Kade joined her, sliding an arm around her waist. "You okay?"

"Yeah. Tired." She looked around the room, her gaze pausing at each of the Hell Hounds. "I just want to go home."

Ronan crossed the room to stand in front of her. "Not yet. I've got a job for you to do." He headed for the closest Hell Hound, glancing over his shoulder to her. "Well?"

Sighing, Amber joined him, staring down at the hound. It was the one she'd helped kill. "What?"

He held out a piece of paper that had been folded into quarters. *"If you speak one word, I will take you to the crypt and leave you there without a Pliethin."*

Recalling how he'd said he wouldn't show the Knights any weakness earlier she guessed she wasn't about to appreciate what was written on the paper. Reluctantly taking it, she unfolded the paper, reading over the words. Her anger grew as she read through the lines that covered a third of the page. Reaching the end she shoved the paper back at him.

"Burn it." Ronan continued to hold the piece of paper out.

Calling a fireball to her hand, Amber smiled slightly as she pushed it against the paper, hoping it burned Ronan too. It burst into flames and Ronan dropped it to the ground. *"What are you waiting for?"*

Sensing Rian and Daray come closer, Amber waved them back. She crouched by the hound, wrapping her hand around the still warm arm, pressing the fingers of her other hand into the Pliethin cage. Shuffling backwards slightly she moved into the Void, watching as Kade stepped forward, stopping just before he reached where she was. She was relieved he didn't step through her. It was one of the worst feelings.

Looking down at the hound she concentrated on trying to follow the instructions Ronan had given her. It took several minutes to find the pathway. Still holding onto the hound's arm, she searched for more threads. There were none. And the one leading to this Hell Hound was slowly fading. But if the rest of the mages could learn how to do this than they wouldn't be caught unprepared.

She couldn't see why they'd be unable to. Dragon Mages had been able to do it centuries ago. With the help of their dragon, who would take them into the Void, they would choose the pathway leading to the Hell Hound and their dragon would take them to it. Shuffling back slightly, she came out of the Void, bringing the hound with her. Rising to her feet she glanced towards the kitchen wanting to wash her hands again.

Chait picked up the Hell Hound and disappeared into the Void.

"If you're planning on using it to teach the other mages, you better hurry. The thread is fading," Amber said.

"Rian, take Crystal and organise the rest of the mages." Ronan turned to Alsandair. "Return Cooper and Miles to the castle, let the army know to remain on standby, then return here."

Simon and Hannah joined them. After cutting off Hannah's complaints, Simon said, "There's no need to keep your army here. I'm ready to go with you."

Ronan reached for Simon. Amber beat him to it, grabbing his other arm. "I'm sure I can offer him more comfortable accommodations than you. Besides, the Knights already know where I live."

Ronan held her gaze for a moment before he let go of Simon's arm. His gaze fell on Simon. "Jonah and Wayne are in my care. Don't forget that." Ronan disappeared into the Void.

Amber doubted he'd left the area. "Are you ready to come with me now?"

Hannah said no at the same time as Simon nodded. Hannah grabbed Simon's arm, glaring at Amber. "If anything happens to him."

"Don't come after him and nothing will." Amber glanced towards Kade and nodded at the question in his eyes. Pushing her fingers into the Pliethin cage, she stepped into the Void taking Simon with her. She drew the thread of the pathway to the planning room to her, stepping out of the Void before she could be pushed from it. She let go of Simon's arm.

Both Kade and Daray arrived in the room.

"Can I see Jonah?"

Amber shook her head. "Not now. Maybe tomorrow. Daray will show you to one of the guest bedrooms. Let him know if you need anything."

"*I am to watch over you, not your captives,*" Daray said directly to Amber.

"*I have others who can do that. I'm not planning to go*

anywhere other than bed. Well, after I wash. I don't want anything to happen to Simon before we've had a chance to talk to him."

Daray nodded and reached for Simon.

Simon stepped away from him. "I can walk."

Daray grinned. "The Void is quicker and you'll be less likely to make a map of it." Again he reached for Simon, this time managing to take him through the Void.

Amber checked the location Daray had taken Simon to before she turned to Kade, sighing. "I feel like I could sleep for a week."

"I doubt Ronan will let you."

"So do I." She reached for Kade, linking her blood stained fingers through his before she took them through the Void to their bedroom.

Chapter Twenty-Three

The first thing Simon did when he saw Amber the next morning was ask to see Jonah again.

"Can't we at least have breakfast first?"

Kade grinned. "You don't want to see her when she gets really hungry. It tends to bring out the wild animal in her."

"You are not in the least bit funny." Amber grabbed hold of Simon's hand and using her caged Pliethin took him to the dining room where breakfast waited.

Simon drew away from her. "It's manners to ask first."

"Probably." Sitting at the table, she wondered what Ronan would say if she said that to him next time he shifted her through the Void without her permission. She doubted he'd be impressed.

Simon sat across from Amber and Kade. "Can I see Jonah and Wayne after breakfast?"

Finishing her mouth full of toast, Amber said, "I have to talk to Ronan first." She sent him a text with Simon's request while she ate her breakfast. It didn't take long for his reply to come through. *I'll bring Jonah and Wayne and meet you in the planning room in half an hour.*

When she told him, Simon nodded and returned to his breakfast, remaining quiet throughout the rest of the meal. Once they'd eaten, Amber took Simon through the Void to the planning room to wait for Ronan. Kade stayed with them.

Ronan arrived on time. With him came Chait bringing Jonah and Anrai bringing Wayne. Both Knights had their hands chained with the grey shackles. They were used to deaden dragon abilities, but Amber guessed that the difficulty in breaking the metal would make it harder for the Knights to escape.

Jonah pulled away from Chait to face Simon. "They have Martin."

"That's not good." Simon turned to Amber. "Martin is a member of the more fanatical part of our organisation. Do they know you have him?"

Amber shrugged. "I wouldn't have a clue, but he's probably safer with us. Particularly since he admitted to killing off some Knights who asked one too many questions."

"He'd never do that," Wayne said.

"You're time's nearly up. You need to go back into the Void so no one can track you down," Ronan said.

"Are you both unharmed?" Simon looked from one to the other.

Jonah shrugged, glancing towards Ronan. "We'll live." He paused. "Who's taking care of things while you're here?"

"Hannah."

"Are you crazy?" Jonah demanded.

"Who else was I meant to leave in charge? Frederick?"

Amber started to ask who Frederick was when Ronan spoke. "Time's up."

When Simon protested Amber bit back her own. She had more questions she wanted to ask Jonah. Although she doubted he'd answer them. Both him and Wayne had remained silent, just like Stanley and Martin. They were starting to get a collection of prisoners and she had no idea what to do with them.

"I didn't even get to tell him that the binding's been broken," Simon said. "It changes everything."

"Like what?" Amber asked.

"The whole reason for the existence of our group

was to protect the binding and keep it going. Now," Simon shrugged, "I don't have a clue what we're meant to be doing."

"Why does he need to know?" Amber asked.

"Because he's my adviser."

Kade chuckled and Ronan made a sound of disbelief. Amber didn't blame them. She was pretty certain Jonah was far more important than an adviser. "Try again. You keep lying to us and the talk is ended."

"Our policy is not to talk, but well," Simon shrugged again, "the binding has been broken."

"It was useless anyway," Amber said.

"It was protecting the human race from extinction."

"Now the human race has us," Kade said.

Amber laughed when Simon looked towards Ronan. "Oh, not him. The Dragon Mages and a handful of Golds."

"That won't be enough. How are you meant to protect the entire world?" Simon asked.

Amber glanced towards Ronan, not sure how much he wanted Simon to know.

"We'll always have two Dragon Mages watching from the Void for Hell Hound arrivals. They'll be changed every hour so they remain alert during their watch." Then Ronan said to Amber and Kade, *"Which is why you're going to need to recruit more mages."*

Amber wanted to argue, but remembering some of the crazy people they'd found, she nodded. She didn't know that she trusted anyone else to make certain of the sanity of each person they asked to be a mage.

"The caged Pliethins you stole will wear out pretty quickly if you use them all the time," Simon said.

"A Gold Warrior is taking them into the Void. That's where Knight Mages are at a disadvantage. The Dragon Mages have dragon allies, what do you lot have?" Ronan asked.

"After everything that has happen between our two races, I doubt that either side could trust the other," Simon said.

"Dragons always know that today's enemies may very well be tomorrow's allies," Kade said.

Simon looked confused. "You forgive them?"

Ronan grinned. "Of course not. But we are patient."

"How can you expect us to trust when you make comments like that?"

"By not thinking like a human," Amber said.

"I am human," Simon said.

"Not completely. You're a Knight Mage." Amber

recalled her grandfather's rejection of her suggestion to become one. "You're a Knight, aren't you?"

Simon nodded.

"Then how can you bring yourself to become what you have? Isn't that against everything the Knights believe in?"

"Some people are called upon to make sacrifices for the greater good."

Ronan made a sound of disbelief again. "And some people make up all sorts of excuses to feel better about the choices they have to make."

"This conversation isn't solving anything. I came here to discuss what to do about the Hell Hounds. I swore an oath to protect humans. Breaking the binding doesn't change that. I will still continue to protect them."

"As I said earlier, we have mages watching for Hell Hounds. There's an area organised that we hope our Golds can take the hounds to so they can be fought without endangering humans unnecessarily." Ronan grinned. "They tend to get in the way and make a battle more difficult than it needs to be."

"Then what do you want with me? It sounds like you've got it all figured out. Why would you need the Knights?" Simon asked.

"Because we're certain there'll be times when

dozens of hounds come through. If there are too many for us to fight, we need to know who will help," Amber said.

"I can't speak for all the Knights."

"Who can?" Ronan asked.

"No one person. This needs to be discussed amongst the leaders of the Knights."

"How long will it take you to arrange a meeting between your leaders?" Kade asked.

"You would need to let your prisoners go first," Simon said.

"Wayne isn't a leader." At least she hoped he wasn't.

"No, but it wouldn't be fair to leave any behind when negotiating for the release of the others."

"Martin isn't a leader anymore." Amber grinned. "He was dethroned."

"In what way?" Simon asked.

"He's no longer High Protector of Queensland." She enjoyed saying that, not that she was much happier with her grandfather being the new High Protector. Particularly with his hate of dragons.

"That doesn't matter, he still has high standing with the Knight Mages."

"I bet it matters to him." Amber's grin remained in place. When Simon didn't comment, she asked,

"How can he be a Knight Mage when he's never held a Pliethin?"

"There are years of training before a Knight can take the next step and become a Knight Mage."

Amber wondered how old Simon was. She guessed it had to be a lot older than the thirty years he appeared to be. "And what if we refuse to release your people? I mean, Martin isn't even exactly our prisoner. We're just keeping an eye on him for his true captors."

"We are human. We don't have the dragons' pragmatic approach to enemies and allies. We'd need you to release all three of our people before we could even think about fighting at your side."

Amber inclined her head, not bothering to mention Stanley. "We'll discuss it. But I can't promise anything."

"Can I return home while we wait for your answer?"

"No." Amber opened the planning room door and gestured for Daray to enter. "Daray will continue to look after you while you're here."

Daray pushed away from the hallway wall he leaned against and crossed the room, reaching for Simon.

Simon took a step back, holding up his hand to signal stop. "Wait. Why did you heal Ira?"

"Because I'm a healer." They weren't the first words that came to mind. Those words were a complaint about all the continual questions people had for her.

"That isn't an answer."

Amber shrugged. "It's all the answer you'll get because I don't have another one." She nodded towards Daray who grasped Simon's arm and took him into the Void. She couldn't help wondering if Simon told Daray that he needed to learn some manners.

Chapter Twenty-Four

The next couple of days passed quickly. Ronan and Flinn argued against letting the prisoners go free while everyone else thought it would be a good idea to have more warriors on their side. Charles, Amos and Eliza wanted Martin given to them rather than letting him go, but Isaac said to return Martin to the Knight Mages. Roy told Amber that the Knights were splitting apart into separate groups and he didn't have a clue how everything was going to turn out. Even the Knights overseas were being affected by the discovery of Knight Mages and Hell Hounds.

They let Simon return early to his people to find out what they'd do if the three Knights were returned to them and Amber impatiently waited for an answer. When it finally came, not everyone was happy with the decision.

It was Friday, nearly a week since the binding

had been broken, before they met in the courtyard of Temolae Keep. Simon, along with Hannah and a Knight Mage he introduced as Frederick, waited silently for Ronan to arrive. Amber, with Kade on one side, Rian on the other, wondered if she should call him. She wasn't about to let him play games and have them all waiting around for ages.

Ronan stepped out of the Void, his Golds stepping out after him bringing Martin, Jonah, Wayne and Stanley. No one had yet asked for Stanley. Amber had convinced Ronan, after hours of argument, that it was time to give him back too.

Amber indicated Stanley with a wave of her hand. "He was taken prisoner the first time we captured Wayne and Jonah."

"He's not one of ours." Simon barely gave Stanley a glance.

"He's a Knight, from the Brisbane Headquarters," Amber said.

Simon turned to Frederick. "I guess that makes him yours."

"Martin?" Frederick asked.

Martin shook his head. "There was never any plan for him to become a Knight Mage."

Frederick strode forward, pulling Martin from

Chait's grip. "Looks like he's your problem then, Simon." Frederick and Martin vanished.

Simon gestured Hannah forward. "Take Wayne home." He removed the caged Pliethin that hung at his belt, holding it out to Jonah.

As Hannah and Wayne vanished, Jonah stepped forward. He took the Pliethin, hanging it at his neck. "What have you done, Simon?"

"We're allies for the next six months. You would have done the same."

"What does that mean exactly?" Jonah turned to Amber.

"That you help us fight the Hell Hounds and don't retaliate against us, encourage others to attack us or harm us in any way," Amber said.

"But we can do that after the six months are over?" Jonah asked.

Amber laughed at the disbelief she heard in his voice. "Not quite." She dredged up the words Ronan had spoken during one of their many meetings. "On the last day of those six months we meet and discuss where we go from there. If we remain allies, part company as neutral parties or become enemies." She hoped it was the first option, although Ronan believed it would be the last. But he always believed that about everyone.

"All the Knight Mages?"

Simon shook his head at Jonah's question. "Only our group. Fredrick wants no part of the dragons."

"Will you honour the bargain?" Ronan asked.

Jonah looked to each of them, his gaze finally settling on Ronan. "It was made in my name, I will keep it." His hand reached for the Pliethin hanging at his neck.

"What about Stanley?" Amber asked.

"He's not our problem." Jonah looked at Simon. "Is that everything?"

Simon nodded before he faced Amber. "Ring me when they come." Both Knight Mages vanished.

Ronan eyed Stanley with one of his predatory grins. "Looks like no one wants you." He looked Stanley up and down. "Can't say as I blame them."

Seeing Stanley's expression go from shock to rage at Ronan's words, Amber stepped forward. "Leave him be."

Stanley struggled to get away from Alsandair's grip. "I don't need you to speak for me."

She ignored the anger in his voice. "What will you do if we let you go?"

"Return to the Knights. Not the ones that were just here. They aren't true Knights."

Amber wondered if she should tell him about all the changes that had happened while he'd been gone.

Ronan chuckled. "Take him back to the headquarters."

"No." She decided she couldn't let him go without telling him.

"You're going to keep me here? Then why did you bother asking me what I'd do?"

"I'm not going to keep you here. I thought you should know what's been happening while you were gone. There's been changes," Amber said.

"Why do you think I'd believe anything you have to say?" Stanley snarled.

Amber stared at him for a moment, pushing away the anger his words made flare. Shrugging, she met Alsandair's gaze. "Take him back to the headquarters. No need to wait around and see that he makes it to the door." Obviously he didn't need her help.

Kade slid an arm around her waist. "This will give us more time to find the next lot of humans to become mages."

She wanted to protest, but he was right. And it was something that couldn't be put off. She glanced first to Daray before her gaze came to rest on Rian. "Kade and I will go after lunch. Just the two of us."

"Make sure you call Daray if you need help." Rian

disappeared into the Void the moment Amber nodded.

"When you have another twenty or thirty organised, let me know." Ronan vanished before Amber could answer.

Holding out a hand, she threaded her fingers through Kade's when he took it, taking them to the dining room. Lunch was brought in several minutes after she was seated. As soon as they were finished, they returned to the human world to recruit more mages.

By Monday night they'd found twenty humans and agreed to turn five humans that Kade's mother, Kiani, had brought to them, into Dragon Mages. Amber wondered if she should again ask her grandfather if he wanted to be a Knight Mage. Too tired to think about it properly she told Kade she was heading to bed.

He drew her close, kissing her. When he pulled back to stare down at her, he ran a finger across the shadows under one of her eyes. "I won't be long and I'll head to bed too. How about we sleep in tomorrow and have the day off? We can go back to searching on Wednesday."

"Sounds good." She kissed him one last time before

she drew away and stepped into the Void, heading to their bedroom.

Amber fell asleep immediately, to be woken by her phone ringing when she was far from rested. She reached for it, trying to focus on the bright screen.

"Answer it," Kade growled.

The screen said the contact was Hound Emergency. Sleepiness faded as adrenaline kicked in. "This is it." She answered the call. "Yes?"

"They're coming. I've already informed Ronan."

"Let Simon know as well." When the mage agreed, Amber hung up, checking the time before she rose from the bed. She'd barely had an hour's sleep. She stared at Kade for a moment. "The hounds are coming." This time she didn't hear an echo of Vikki as she spoke the words. She felt both nervous and excited. It looked like their plan to watch for the Hell Hounds was working.

Kade got out of bed, pulled on a vest that matched his trousers and armed himself. Amber grabbed her weapons then held out her hand to him. She tightened her fingers on his.

"Are you ready?"

Kade nodded. "More than. Let's go see how many are coming."

Pressing her fingers to the caged Pliethin she'd

hung at her belt, she took them into the Void, searching for the pathway to the Hell Hounds. It only took her seconds to find and she pulled it to herself.

"You know I think I could follow this thread back to their world. It's much stronger and clearer than the one from the hound we killed."

"Not on your own."

Amber grinned. "You aren't going to tell me I can't do it?"

"No. Being able to get some of their stone to protect our castle better would be worth the risk."

"Sounds like a plan." She tightened her fingers on his before she took them through the Void. They stepped out into a crowd of Golds and warriors, the ones at the outside of the crowd unarmed. The concrete footpath she stood on was cracked and uneven, leading to closed shops that continued on past the crowd. She had no idea where she was, but that wasn't important. Getting the Hell Hounds out of here the moment they arrived was.

Familiar faces were everywhere Amber looked. Including Crystal, Rian, Jasper, Turi, Angela and Flinn. She couldn't see any Knight Mages or Ronan, but she could feel the waves of fear rising. The Hell Hounds weren't far away. Ronan better hurry up.

Crystal covered the short distance between them, throwing her arms around her. "I hope this works."

Amber hugged Crystal tightly before letting her go. "Of course it will." She doubted Ronan would accept anything else.

Simon, Jonah and Hannah stepped out of the Void, along with three other Knight Mages. Simon nodded towards Amber in greeting, the rest of the Knight Mages barely giving her a glance. Ronan and six Golds stepped out of the Void in front of her and Amber wondered if the Knight Mages' arrival had been what they'd been waiting for.

Ronan grinned. "Ready, kitten?"

"Yes." The fear was increasing by the second. She knew the Hell Hounds were only minutes away.

The moment two Hell Hounds appeared, Amber raced towards the one that Ronan grabbed. Holding onto its arm, she nodded towards Ronan and they forced it into the Void. It nearly escaped her grip. Through the haze of the Void she saw all the unarmed warriors and Golds press in towards the group that was vanishing into the Void to make it harder for humans to notice what was going on. The other Hell Hound wasn't visible and Amber guessed that Simon and Jonah were doing their part of the plan. For a moment she wished she had Crystal's ability to see who was in the Void so she'd know for sure that the other Hell Hound hadn't escaped.

"Hurry and shift," Ronan said.

Amber waited until she had a better grip on the Hell Hound before she nodded and they took him through the Void to a large shed on a dilapidated farm that Ronan had found west of Brisbane. Jumping back, she drew her sword, attacking the Hell Hound. Around her Golds brought warriors and mages out of the Void.

Jonah and Simon came out of the Void with the other Hell Hound. She didn't have time to see how they were doing, she was too busy dodging the claws that came for her.

The Hell Hound roared, turning on Kade who attacked from behind. Seeing the hound was momentarily distracted, Amber called flames to her blade, stabbing it into him. It went into his side as he'd started to turn towards her. Jasper raced towards them, his own blade flaming. Angela was with him, lightning crackling along her blade.

Amber dodged to the left, drawing her daggers as she did, calling flames to the blades. They all attacked together. Kade, Ronan and the other Golds with them, while Amber, Jasper and Angela drove their weapons into the hound. He roared, crashing to the ground.

Checking for Crystal, she found her and Rian attacking the other Hell Hound, along with the Knight Mages. The hound glanced towards his dead companion, roaring and attacking harder. She wanted to join the fight against the last hound, but she'd only get in the way. He was already surrounded. Reaching for his mind, she found it was like reaching for the mind of a wyvern, only more filled with hate. She quickly let go and checked for anyone who might have been wounded in the fight.

Everyone was fine other than a handful of cuts and bruises. The last hound crashed to the ground and Jonah withdrew his sword from the creature, looking towards Amber. He held her gaze for a moment, then nodded before he disappeared into the Void. The rest of the Knight Mages left, only Simon remaining to stride towards Amber.

She waited for him, taking her weapons that Kade held out to her. Checking Simon over, she saw only a bruise on his jaw. Nothing worth worrying about. And not anywhere near bad enough to risk weakening him with dragon blood to heal it. "All your people are fine?"

Simon nodded. "Your plan might work."

"It's Ronan's." Her gaze was drawn to Ronan, who joined them.

"It's what should have been done to start with, not the binding," Ronan said.

"We had a lot of years of peace from them because of the binding," Simon said.

"At what cost?"

Amber wondered if he'd lost someone to the Knight Mages. A friend or a lover who'd been sacrificed to maintain the binding. Maybe she'd ask him later. Seeing his hard expression, she decided that if she did, it would be much later, if at all.

"I will wait to hear from you." Simon reached for his caged Pliethin.

"Simon." She waited for him to drop his hand. "Jonah's your leader, isn't he?"

"No. We share that task." He looked like he was about to say something, then stopped. Reaching for the Pliethin, he nodded towards them and vanished.

"I'm heading home," Jasper said. "Isleen is waiting up for me."

"Okay." She watched as her brother and Turi disappeared.

Crystal joined them, Rian at her side. "That wasn't as bad as the first time. When we fought them that time I was so terrified I could barely attack."

"You'll get used to the fear they cause." Ronan paused. "Or you'll die."

"She will not die," Rian said.

Ronan looked from one to the other before he turned to Amber. "When were you going to tell me?"

"I wasn't. It's not up to me."

Ronan pointed his finger at Rian. "I want to see you at my place first thing this morning." He glanced towards Amber before facing Rian again. "Before breakfast." He vanished into the Void.

Amber laughed. "That'd probably be my fault that he expects you to visit before breakfast."

Angela joined them, yawning. "I don't know about you lot, but we're heading home. Just about everyone's gone anyway."

Amber reached for Angela as Flinn took hold of her hand. "You're okay?" She couldn't smell any blood, but that didn't mean Angela was unhurt.

"Yeah." Angela grinned. "I wish you could have told me sooner. This is the life I was training for."

"I'm glad." When she let go of Angela, Flinn took her into the Void.

Kade held out his hand. "Home?"

Amber glanced around. Nearly everyone was gone. Only a handful of Golds were left. With a smile towards Crystal, she stepped close to Kade and his arm encircled her. "Yeah, let's go home."

When they came out of the Void, she did a quick search and found Angela and Flinn already there, Crystal and Rian arriving seconds later. Tiredness hit her and she unsuccessfully tried to hold back a yawn. "I need a wash. Then I'm going to sleep until late afternoon."

Kade chuckled. "Let's hope that this time it works."

Poking her tongue out at him, she headed for the bathroom. As soon as she'd showered, Amber dropped onto the bed, lying awake while she tried to get her mind to turn off. She was tired, but she couldn't stop thinking. In the end, she decided she'd see her grandparents after she woke. Give them another chance at becoming Knight Mages. Maybe with all the changes that had occurred in the Knights' organisation, they might be interested.

Chapter Twenty-Five

Late the next morning Amber stared at the blank screen of her phone, wondering if her grandfather was going to reply to her text. She was just about to give up when one came through. *We're at home. Going out in thirty.*

Searching for Kade, she used the Pliethin to take her to the room he was in. She paused to watch him train against Brann. When they stopped and Kade looked in her direction, she smiled. "Want to visit my grandfather?"

Kade sheathed his sword as he strode towards her. "I thought you were going to sleep in."

"I was, but you were supposed to as well. I woke up and you were gone."

"Miss me?"

She slid her arms around his waist. "Maybe." She kissed him, her arms tightening around him, his going around her. Eventually she drew back to meet his gaze. "Well? You want to come with me? They're going out soon."

"Sure."

Amber laughed. "Try not to sound so enthusiastic." Keeping one arm around him, she pressed her fingers into the Pliethin cage, taking them to the front of her grandparent's house. Letting go of Kade she knocked on the door.

When she sensed someone come out of the Void behind her, she spun towards them, her hand going for her sword that hung at her side. She wasn't fast enough. They dragged her into the Void as the front door opened and Kade reached for her. She struggled to escape from the Knight Mage, smelling in his blood what he was.

They came out in a study with an antique desk and floor to ceiling bookcases, Martin and Fredrick in front of her. She pulled away from the man who'd held her, reaching for her caged Pliethin. The man grabbed her arm, twisting it behind her back.

Ignoring the pain, Amber demanded of Martin, "What do you want?"

"I want what should have been done ages ago." He stepped close to her.

She held her ground, meeting his gaze. "And what's that?"

Martin slowly smiled, taking the last step between them. "This."

Pain exploded through her, before a kind of numbness settled in. She looked down to see a dagger, still held by Martin, pushed into her stomach. The man holding her arm let go and she grabbed Martin as her legs started to give way. Looking up her vision was filled with Martin's satisfied smile. Plunging her fingers into the Pliethin cage she dragged him back into the Void with her, taking him to Ronan's crypt. It was a struggle to remain standing and when Martin pulled from her grasp, she staggered back into the wall, starting to slide down it. She could barely hold onto consciousness. Ronan would eventually find Martin and her people would be safe from him.

Ronan stepped out of the Void. "I warned-" He broke off, drawing his sword, swinging at Martin.

Sitting on the floor, Amber pulled the dagger out, the world starting to recede even further. She pressed her hands against the wound, trying to focus on healing.

"Kitten."

Meeting Ronan's gaze, she reached out a hand to

touch his cheek. "I'm sorry." The other hand she kept pressed against the wound, still trying to heal herself.

"Hold on." He gripped her shoulders.

She tried to speak again, but the world felt like it caved in on her bringing with it blackness.

* * *

She heard sobbing before she was properly awake. "Mum?" Amber struggled to open her eyes, gasping as she tried to sit up in the bed.

"Don't you dare move."

She finally managed to open her eyes to see Ronan standing over her, blood still staining his cheek. Her blood. "Thirsty."

He moved out of her view, returning seconds later with a glass, a bendable straw in it. "Only a little."

A little wasn't going to help with how thirsty she was, but Ronan pulled the straw away before she'd drunk much. She opened her mouth to protest.

"Finish healing yourself first."

She slid a hand under the blanket, finding a bandage wrapped around her middle. Before she could do anything, Ronan reached out and lifted her arm so her bracelets were in her view. With a nod, she drew power from some of them before she tried to heal herself. It was harder than she'd expected, but finally she could sit up. Glancing around the room she saw her mother nearby. Gary stood with her, an arm around her shoulders.

"You want to tell me what happened?" Ronan demanded.

"A Knight Mage came out of the Void when I went to visit my grandparents. He took me to Martin and Fredrick. What happened-" Breaking off, she glanced towards her mother who was still sobbing. "When I ahh…" she avoiding saying collapsed. Not wanting her mother to hear the word. "What happened to Martin?"

"I told you what would happen to anyone you brought there. Did you forget?"

"No." She held his gaze a moment. "I remembered." Then she spoke directly to him. *"How did you manage to arrive so quickly? I didn't expect that."*

"I know the moment anyone enters the crypt."

"How."

"You aren't capable of doing it."

"Is Kade?"

Ronan stared at her for nearly a minute. *"Maybe one day."*

She wanted to ask him all the details, but decided now wasn't the time. *"What'll we do about Fredrick?"*

"He will suffer the same fate as Martin."

Once she would have protested. Her hand continued to rest against the place the dagger had been. It wasn't a game. It never had been. It was survival of the fittest and she wasn't about to let someone else win. She had too much to live for. *"Okay."*

Ronan held out a dagger to her.

She eyed it, certain it was the one Martin had stabbed her with.

"Take it."

"Why?"

"To the winner go the spoils."

She took the dagger, sliding it under her pillow.

Ronan smiled. "I'll let Kade know he can visit you now." He vanished.

Donna broke away from Gary, still sobbing, to stand at Amber's bedside. "I thought you were dead. When he brought you in, I thought you were dead. There was so much blood."

"I'll be okay, Mum."

"You said me becoming a mage could keep you safe. It can't. You nearly died because you're a mage."

"No, I said becoming a mage could keep you safe."

Irritation and anger began to rise. "Do we have to do this? I'm fine." Why had Ronan brought her to her mother? She'd have a talk to him about that.

Kade stepped out of the Void. "I tried to grab you before he took you away." He lifted her hand, his fingers tightening on hers.

"I know. I saw you."

"Ronan said Fredrick was involved."

"Yeah. He was with Martin."

"Then he's dead," Kade said flatly.

Ronan came out of the Void with Simon. Both looked angry. Ronan pushed Simon towards Amber. "Tell him, kitten. Tell him who was there."

"Fredrick."

"I had no idea he planned this," Simon said.

"Then what are you going to do about it?" Ronan demanded.

"Can I speak to Amber? Alone?" Simon asked.

Amber looked around the room. Kade shook his head, Ronan's expression remained neutral and Gary had his arm around her mother again. Her gaze came to a stop on Simon. "Okay."

"Are you sure?" Ronan asked Amber directly.

"Yeah." She waited until everyone was out of the room before she spoke to Simon. "What did you want to talk about?"

"We don't want this affecting our partnership. Jonah and I were talking about making it long term. We can't look for the Hell Hounds like Dragon Mages can. And we might not like dragons, but we have nothing against those who are willing to help humans. That's what we're about. The protection of the human race."

"What are you going to do about Fredrick?"

"I won't help you kill him if that's what you expect, but we have broken completely away from their group. Even if our partnership should end tomorrow, we would still have nothing to do with them."

"Why?"

"Because they've forgotten the reason we were formed."

"Okay."

"Does that mean things are still good between us?"

Amber nodded. "Yeah, things are still good. We'll call you when the next lot of Hell Hounds arrive."

"Thank you." He glanced over his shoulder. "Can I go now?"

"I'll check." She reached for Ronan who wasn't far from the room. *"Simon's not to be held accountable for Fredrick's actions. Can he go now?"*

Ronan appeared in the room. "You don't plan to assist him in any way?"

Simon shook his head. "Their group has nothing to do with ours."

"You can go then." When Simon left, Ronan stepped close to the bed. "You're going to have to stop doing this, kitten. You need to take more care."

"I survived, didn't I?"

Ronan stared down at her a moment longer before he grinned. "Yeah. Make sure you continue to."

She nodded. "Why did you bring me to my mother?"

"I didn't. I brought you to Gary."

That made more sense. "Thanks."

"When you're better, you can help me track down Fredrick."

"I don't know him that well. Not to be able to track him over long distances."

Ronan stared at her silently. He nodded. "We'll find another way to find him."

"Okay."

Ronan held her gaze a moment longer before he vanished into the Void.

She stared at the place he'd been for several minutes before she called to Kade, asking him to join her. When he arrived, she tugged him close. "We've still got to see my grandparents."

"Maybe we should suggest them coming to see you."

Amber shook her head. "No. I'm not about to cower and hide. We will go and see them."

"Now?"

She shook her head. "In a day or two." When she was feeling a lot better.

"Okay."

She grinned at the unenthusiastic tone he used.

Chapter Twenty-Six

Amber sprawled on the carpet in front of the television, not having heard most of the movie that she, Crystal, Angela and Maira were supposedly watching. It was almost like old times. Except instead of being at her parent's house, they were in her house that Jasper lived in. They would have had their movie night at Temolae Keep except that the dragon world wasn't that good with electronics. Regular bursts of static didn't make watching movies much fun.

And back before she'd met Kade, Angela hadn't played with lightning, sliding it through her fingers like it was a cat winding its way in and out and around them. Nor did they have weapons lying within arm's reach. Amber smiled. There were some differences, but the main things hadn't changed. Her friends and family. She had more friends and certainly more family, but they were all still important to her.

Crystal threw a cushion at Amber who caught it before it hit her. "What did you do that for?"

"Because I asked you twice what you were thinking about. You weren't paying any attention to me."

"Everything." She smiled. "I still can't believe it'll be a year tomorrow since we captured Temolae Keep."

"I can't believe you turned down a ball to celebrate," Crystal said. "Well, I can believe, but you could have said yes. I'd love to have another ball."

Before she had a chance to reply, her phone rang and she smiled when she saw the display read Hound Emergency. "Yeah?"

"The hounds are coming."

"Who else has been notified?"

"Ronan, Jonah and Charles."

"Okay. We'll be right there." Amber hung up as she sensed Kade and Rian enter the house, striding towards the room they were in. "Time to go. Hell Hounds."

Crystal rose to her feet, grabbing her sword and complaining.

Angela grinned. "I hope more come through this time. Six was a breeze. I want them to send ten. Maybe then it'd be a bit of a challenge."

"Going to their world and bringing back some of their stone wasn't enough of a challenge for you?" Amber asked, glancing towards Kade as he entered the room with Rian.

"Nope."

Kade chuckled. "Then you'll be glad to know Ronan's planning another trip."

"Awesome." Angela looked from Kade to Amber. "Who's giving me a lift? Or am I waiting for Flinn?" She was still trying to learn how to use the caged Pliethins.

"Me," Kade said. "We're going to the location the hounds will arrive at. Flinn will meet you at the farm."

"Guess Maira's stuck with me." Amber held out her hand, which Maira took. "I'll meet everyone there."

It didn't take her long to find the pathway to where the Hell Hounds would arrive this time. They came out in a forest. Several people held torches, the only light in the area. The overhead branches prevented any starlight or moonlight from reaching the ground. Charles and Helen came out of the Void nearby, a caged Pliethin hung from his belt. This would be his first battle as a Knight Mage. It had been Jonah who'd convinced him to become a Knight Mage, nothing she'd said had helped.

Ronan came out of the Void beside her. "Ready, kitten?"

She nodded, knowing the hounds had to be close with how strong the waves of terror were. "Yeah." She stepped forward with him when the hound appeared in front of them, taking it through the Void to the farm, jumping back out of the way as it attacked.

Drawing her sword, she sensed Knight Mages bring the other four hounds into the building. Maybe one day the hounds would no longer fall for them transporting them here the moment they arrived on Earth, but for now it worked and they'd continue to use it.

She brought flames to her blade, attacking the hound, driving the sword into him, turning into a goshawk to fly out of reach of his claws as he howled. Landing behind him, she drew her daggers. Kade was on one side of her, Crystal on the other, Jasper nearby. Flames burst from her blades and she grinned.

It had taken her a while to figure it out, but this was her life. Ronan had been right. Her daggers sank into the hound at the same time as Crystal and Kade's swords did. The hound crashed to the ground with a final roar. Her gaze met Kade's and she smiled. Her heart was racing, her senses alert.

She was a warrior. And she was going to survive.

Free Ebook

Subscribe to Avril's newsletter and receive a free ebook. This ebook is exclusive to those on her mailing list. To find out more about this offer visit:

www.avrilsabine.com/free-ebook

*

We value your privacy and will not sell, rent, exchange or loan your email address to third parties. Your information is confidential and you are under no obligation to remain on the mailing list and can unsubscribe at any time.

Acknowledgements

As always, thanks to the usual crew. I couldn't manage without you.

To The Reader

If you enjoyed this book, why not consider leaving a review to help other readers discover it too? Reader engagement is one of the few ways that lets an author know readers want more books in a particular series or genre. So leave a review and tell friends, not only about this book but also about other ones you've enjoyed, so you can continue to enjoy books by your favourite authors for years to come.

Dreams are meant to be lived,

Avril.

About The Author

Avril is an Australian author who lives with her family on acreage in South East Queensland. She writes mostly young adult and children's speculative fiction, but has been known to dabble in other genres. You can find more information about her at www.avrilsabine.com where you can also subscribe to her newsletter to be kept informed about new releases, current projects, blog posts and exclusive news.

Titles By Avril Sabine

Stories about strong characters and characters who discover their strengths.

SERIES

Assassins Of The Dead- Young Adult Fantasy/ Paranormal

Book 1: Dark Blade

Book 2: Dragon Touched

Book 3: Society Against Vampires

Book 4: King's Request

Dragon Blood- Young Adult Urban Fantasy (with elements of romance)

(5 book series)

Book 1: Pliethin

Book 2: Wyvern

Book 3: Surety

Book 4: Knight

Book 5: Mage

Dragon Mage- Young Adult Urban Fantasy (with elements of romance)

(Series two of Dragon Blood series)

Book 1: Promise

Dragon Blood Chronicles- Young Adult Urban Fantasy (with elements of romance)

(Companion stand alone series to Dragon Blood)

Book 1: Oath

Book 2: Betrayed

Guardians Of The Round Table- Young Adult Fantasy LitRPG

(Co-written with Storm and Rhys Petersen)

Book 1: Dexterity Fail

Book 2: Goblin Boots

Book 3: Singed Feathers

Book 4: Frog Mage

Book 5: Crystal Mine

Book 6: Cursed Harp

Rosie's Rangers- Young Adult Western Steampunk

(6 book series)

Book 1: Justice

Book 2: Vengeance

Book 3: Treachery

Book 4: Accused

Book 5: Wanted

Book 6: Corruption

Mark Of Kings- Children's Fantasy

(Upper middle grade/preteen)

(4 book series)

Book 1: The Arena

Book 2: The Island

Book 3: The Assassin

Book 4: The King

STAND ALONE SERIES

Demon Hunters- Young Adult Urban Fantasy/ Horror (with elements of romance)

Book 1: Blood Sacrifice

Book 2: Retribution

Book 3: Tainted

Book 4: Premonition

Book 5: Cursed

Book 6: Feud

Book 7: Extrication

Plea Of The Damned- Young Adult Urban Fantasy/Paranormal

(6 book series)

Book 1: Forgive Me Lucy

Book 2: Forgive Me Aiden

Book 3: Forgive Me Jena

Book 4: Forgive Me Kobe

Book 5: Forgive Me Marti

Book 6: Forgive Me Dawson

Realms Of The Fae- Young Adult Urban Fantasy (with elements of romance)

The Sword (short story in Like A Girl Anthology)

Heart Of Stone

Book 1: A Debt Owed

Book 2: Marked By The Hunt

Book 3: The Magic Collector

Book 4: An Unexpected Betrayal

Book 5: Imprisoned By Iron

Fairytales Retold (Short Stories)

Snow-White And Rose-Red

The Twelve Brothers

The Light Princess

Beauty And The Beast

Sleeping Beauty

Aschenputtel

The Golden Bird

The Frog Prince

The Death Of Koshchei The Deathless

Myths And Legends Retold (Short Stories)

Ion, Son Of Apollo

Sir Gawain And The Maid With The Narrow Sleeves

Princess Ilse, The Giant's Daughter

YOUNG ADULT NOVELS

Young Adult Fantasy (with elements of romance)

Elf Sight

Earth Bound

Young Adult Urban Fantasy

Stone Warrior (with elements of romance)

The Jungle Inside

Young Adult Contemporary (with elements of romance)

Through Your Eyes

The Ugly Stepsister

Perfect Little Princess

Young Adult Contemporary/Paranormal

Whispers In The Dark (with elements of romance and same sex relationships)

Over Too Soon (with elements of romance)

Young Adult Sci-Fi

Experiment X-One-Six (Urban Sci-Fi/Superheroes)

An Endless Dawn (Post Apocalyptic Sci-Fi)

CHILDREN'S BOOKS

Dragon Lord (Preteen/early teens) (Fantasy)

The Irish Wizard (Upper middle grade) (Urban Fantasy)

SHORT STORIES

Urban Fantasy

Eternally Late

Dealings With Joe

Glimpses (short story in That Moment When Anthology)

Contemporary

The Brat Next Door

Fantasy LitRPG

(Set in the same world as Guardians Of The Round Table Series)

Tales Of Inadon 1: The Disc (Co-written with Storm and Rhys Petersen) (short story in Game On! Anthology)

Post Apocalyptic Sci-Fi

Compulsive Directive

NONFICTION

A Year Of Weekly Writing Exercises (Creative Writing)

Cooking For Families With Allergies (Cooking) (Co-written with Storm Petersen)

Tell Me A Story, Grandma (Memoir)

For the most up to date details on available titles visit:

www.avrilsabine.com/books/bibliography

Dragon Blood Series

To learn more about this series visit:

www.avrilsabine.com/series/db

BOOKS AVAILABLE IN THE DRAGON BLOOD SERIES

(5 book series)

Book 1: Pliethin

Book 2: Wyvern

Book 3: Surety

Book 4: Knight

Book 5: Mage

BOOKS SET IN THE SAME WORLD AS THE DRAGON BLOOD SERIES

Dragon Mage- Young Adult Urban Fantasy (with elements of romance)

(Series two of Dragon Blood series)

Book 1: Promise

Book 2: Pact

Dragon Blood Chronicles- Young Adult Urban Fantasy (with elements of romance)

(Companion stand alone series to Dragon Blood)

Book 1: Oath

Book 2: Betrayed

Disclaimer

This is a work of fiction. Names, characters, businesses, places, events and incidents are either the products of the author's imagination or used in a fictitious manner. Any resemblance to actual persons, living or dead, or actual events is purely coincidental. The opinions expressed or beliefs held are those of the characters and should not be assumed to be the opinions or beliefs of the author.